ruin.

Songs of Corruption – Book Two

Cara Kim
Grazie
CDReiss

CD Reiss   *2014*

Cover Art designed by the author

ruin.

preface.

The mafia. The mob. Cosa nostra. Camorra.
'Ndrangehta. Organized crime.

You'd think you could nail down a little
consistency with organizations that are behind so much
modern-crime folklore.

Alas, organized crime in 2014 bears no
resemblance to versions from the '70s, '80s, or '90s.
The illusion of constancy arises from the mythologies
of the men of tradition running them, not from
historical fact.

But tradition is not the same as uniformity. And the
authorities think they know shit. They don't.
Wikipedia is a joke. I've got books. Each tells a
different story, and all the stories are true. The facts are
not neat and tidy, and the anecdotes are often confused
with universal truth.

So, let's do this instead.

Let's have some fun.

You've met my broken billionaire. My submissive musician. My shattered celebutante. My painful dichotomies. I've introduced you to my family traditions, my honorable pledges, my versions of ambition and art.

Let me introduce you to *my* mob.

This is my Neapolitan camorra. These are my rituals, my sold souls, my men of honor.

This is my Los Angeles.

chapter 1.

THERESA

Everything bled. The sun bled gold over the skyline.
The deep blue horizon bled over the map of the streets.
The trapezoid of light bled across the carpet as the day
passed. The smog bled into the cloud. From the tower,
I presided over silence.

    I didn't know how many hours a day I sat in front
of that window, looking out over the breadth of the Los
Angeles basin with its endless ocean of greys and
browns, wondering where he was and where I was and
how many hours were between us. Wondering if I'd
eaten or if my motionless night at the window had
been cut by sleep or if my open-eyed diligence was to
end in another day of bleeding the hours of life into the
endlessness of death.

He was gone. He didn't talk about what he did, but I was sure the sun draining onto the blanket of the basin was blood shed by him or his men or on his behalf. I feared it was his. Everyone's blood looked the same once spilled, but his, running the same color as a polluted sun, would have brought me to tears.

The most tender symptom of aging is the reduction of choices. I'd wanted to be everything when I was a girl: a scientist, a politician, a financier, a lawyer. But I'd made a choice to be nothing, bleeding options from a wound where my heart had been pulled out, inflated to ten times its normal size, and put back.

Time had passed in that bland grey apartment. People had come and gone, like Zia Giovanna, Antonio's aunt who ran a restaurant in San Pedro, and Zo, one of his associates, a sweet man who had no problem beating the life out of someone. Others with names and accents came, bringing food, clothing, comfort, and I still had no idea how I'd gotten there.

Not physically. I remembered the multiple cars, the handoffs in desolate places. But I couldn't recall the single decision I'd made that had yanked me from my world and into that place, high above the city, where I knew no one, had no connection to the things I'd spent years building, and had no influence on decisions made about my life.

I was able to leave.

People watched me, but I could have eluded them if I'd gotten my mind to wiggle around options and choices. With a well-built strategy for escape, I could have left in a blaze of light or the thick of night. I had a phone. One call to my father, and my confinement would have been over. Or to Daniel. I could manage anything I set my mind to, even if I was watched. And I wasn't being kept against my will. Not really. Not in a way that was decidedly illegal, but only in a way that left me staring at the breadth of the city and out to the horizon, bleeding time.

Until he came.

He barely knocked when he entered. Maybe the *whickCLAP* of the lock should have been as good as a knock. Or the mumbles of him and the guy outside, with his voice an interlocking puzzle piece to something in my brain. Something with needs. Something desperate. But every time he came to the apartment, I was surprised and relieved and hungry, like a woman who was so starved she hadn't even entertained the thought of food until someone slipped a bowl of stew through a flap in the door.

I paused when he closed the door behind him. I never knew which Antonio I was getting when he walked in. It didn't matter if he was in jeans and a polo shirt or, as was the case that day, a jacket and sky-blue turtleneck. He could be any one of ten incarnations.

"Contessa." He tossed his keys on the end table.

I said nothing. Not yet. I was afraid speaking would break the spell, and like that, he'd disappear in a flare.

He shrugged out of his jacket, revealing the brown-leather shoulder holster that creased his sweater. He wore it in my presence. He trusted me. He wasn't afraid, and as he walked toward me, the straps cutting his frame didn't scare me either. The gun made me bold. The scruff on his face and the circles under his eyes made me compassionate, and the line shadows bleeding from his feet to the side of the room in the late sun made me angry.

"Capo," I said when he was a step away.

He gently reached for my cheek, and before he could embrace me and sweep me away, I tilted my body back and slapped his face.

I hit him so hard his neck snapped ninety degrees until he was facing the window. The sound of skin hitting skin rang against the walls.

And I felt not an ounce of regret.

I raised my hand again, and he grabbed the wrist. He was not gentle when he drew it down, nor when he stepped toward me, pushing me back against the table. His breath was hot on me, his body a field of energy. His hips pressed against me so forcefully his erection hurt through my clothes.

"Did you want to tell me something?" Antonio let my wrist go so he could put his hand up my shirt. He shoved my bra out of the way and grabbed a nipple, pinching to pain.

"Where were you?" I gasped the question. All the accusation and anger heated to a sticky, molten mass between my legs.

"It's business."

"God," I groaned. "Go to hell."

I tried to wiggle away, but he grabbed under my arms and threw me on the table. I swung; he dodged and held me down with his weight while peeling my pants off.

"Did you hear me?" I growled.

"I heard you."

I kicked at him, twisting. I fell off the table with a crash, pants halfway down, and I flipped so he wouldn't have me helpless on my stomach. He grabbed my ankle and dragged me across the room. My shirt rolled up, exposing my skin to the burn of the carpet, which matched the burn between my legs.

"You're not understanding your place, Contessa."

He whipped my pants off. In the split second before he grabbed me again, I scuttled to my feet and backed up.

"My place? It's next to you."

"It's under me." He came for me. I slapped him again, hard, the force of my body behind it, but it didn't stop him that time. He took me by the arms and threw me on the couch like a rag doll. I lay there with my legs splayed, my elbows under me, looking up at him with a clenched jaw as he undid his pants.

"Don't you even think about it."

"I'm not thinking about it." He wedged himself between my legs and pushed my knees apart. "I'm doing it."

I slapped him again, twice in the face, three times in the chest, and he ignored all of it as if he were under attack by mosquitoes.

"Fuck you," I said when he slid his cock along my soaked cleft, not entering me but teasing, even as I lashed out at him. I got a good shot to the neck, and he latched my wrists together in two of his fingers, binding me with his flesh.

"Say 'fuck me,'" he said, putting his other hand on my throat.

"Fuck you," I whispered.

He moved his hips, sliding the length of his cock on my clit. He leaned down, and I smelled the burned nicotine on his breath.

"Wrong. Say what you want."

My pussy pulsed for him, and while my hands and shoulders thrust against him, my lower half pushed into him.

"You're hurting me."

He pressed his dick on me harder and hooked his fingers onto the side of my jaw.

"Say it."

"You're garbage." I was clothed in him, a corset laced tight with desire and pain. I wanted his fingers to dig into me and find my filth, my foulness. Only he could find it and grind it out. There was only one way to do that. There had only ever been one way. "Fuck me. Fuck me hard, you worthless piece of shit."

With a twist of his hips, he was right there. I felt him. I moved against him, the slickness of my pussy an open invitation.

"Do it!" I said as loudly as I could manage with his hand on my throat.

"Beg."

"No."

He slid along me again, a strafing of pleasure between my thighs. I moved with him involuntarily, shifting so that worthless and beautiful man would rub me.

"No?" He said it as if he were speaking to a child.

"Fuck you."

"No."

"Please."

"Now we're getting somewhere." He let go of my wrists, and I balled up my fists and pushed against his chest, even as I pushed my hips against him.

"Please, Antonio."

"Please, what?" He unstrapped his gun, letting it drop to the floor in a tangle of leather and iron, and pulled his sweater off.

"Please, fuck me good." I punched his chest. "Fuck me hard. Use me like the punk you are."

He slammed into me, taking my breath away, before I'd even finished the sentence, and time stopped. He had me pinned, and I accepted him, pushing myself against him. It was the only direction I could move in.

"This good, Contessa?" he said in my ear. "This how you want it?"

My mouth was open, but no words came out. Only vowels. With every thrust, a wave of hot-pink pleasure came in, and then another.

"Capo," I groaned. "Fuck."

"Those words," he whispered.

"Destroy me."

"You're ruined, *amore. Rovinata.*"

And at the thought of being left a ruined piece of flesh and bone, I burst into flames of sensation, crying his name, be it Capo, or Antonio, or my own personal dance with death. I claimed him to the heavens.

chapter 2.

ANTONIO

I was taught that a woman needed to be protected. She needed stability. Tenderness. A woman needed to feel safe and build a home for a family. A woman needed a future, a hope of comfort. She needed a man who'd stand between her and danger.

The securest place for Theresa was with her ex, Daniel. I admitted I was already failing to put her in the safest situation, because I'd die before letting him have her.

My father, who ran the entire olive trade in Napoli, never told my mother a thing about how he got his money. He made two children with her. He made her an honest woman. He gave her all the things a woman needs until she threw it back at him because he couldn't leave the business. She threw his name away; she took his children; she made herself the target of contempt. I'd always thought my mother was the one with the broken heart, because my father was a cold, cruel man.

One night when I was maybe eighteen, he came to the mechanic shop, drunk. He didn't drink much, but it was his birthday, and my father did not like birthdays.

I had a Fiat on the lift. Grease up to the elbows at midnight. The customer was demanding, and wanted his car right away. I'd had to leave my father's birthday party to finish the job.

"*Figlio*," he said.

"Papa." I didn't look away from the transmission. It was a tricky thing.

"You have a woman now. You're going to marry her." He'd told me before that he liked Valentina, so I didn't expect he was about to give me trouble about it.

"If her father agrees."

"He will. I'll make sure of it."

"I'd rather win my own way." I always did things my way because it made my mother happy when I was away from my father's influence. But I liked my father; he taught me a lot, and I felt like a man around him.

He sat in silence for a while.

"What's on your mind, Papa?"

"When are you leaving for Milano?"

He was obsessed with my going to law school. He asked a thousand questions about it, how much it cost, how the year was broken up, who my compatriots were. But he never got to the point until that night.

"August," I answered.

"I've talked to every capo. None will take you for their *consigliere*."

"Have you talked to yourself?" I looked away from the car long enough to make eye contact.

And it all became clear right then. He was worried I'd become like him. Even though he watched over me and gave me jobs, he was of two minds. He'd send me on an errand with one hand, because he didn't trust anyone else, and with the other, he'd tell me to go to law school in the north to be away from the *camorra*.

"You will never be my *consigliere*." He tilted his chin up and rocked his hand at the wrist, two fingers up, which he did when he meant to be taken seriously.

"I'll be a prosecutor." I smiled up at the transmission. I had no intention of being a prosecutor or a defender. I wanted to do family law, and he knew it.

"I want you to keep that woman," he said.

"Yes, Pop. *Bene*." My father could have had any woman, but he pined for my mother, who despised him. He'd never change for her or her children. He'd never try and be a man he wasn't. He was a crook and as damned to hell as they came, and he knew it. He'd risk me being a non-*camorra* lawyer for the love of keeping me from being like him.

At the time, it seemed easy. The path was straight and clear. My father taught me how to hold two opposing ideas in my mind at once, but he never taught me how to live those opposites.

How distorted the path must have become, to have gotten me to America. To Los Angeles, of all places. I was neither *consigliere* nor lawful. Neither husband nor free. And now, I was twisted with that red-haired beauty I could never resist or deny. I'd been on a death-march from the minute I saw her, with her porcelain skin and blue eyes. She was a swan, gliding across the floor, so straight that I had to see her bend.

Then I saw that mistake on her shoe, that imperfection inside that perfect package. It was a sign that I could have the unattainable, and when I touched her arm and spoke softly, she bent to hear me. She smelled like sweet olive trees, and she blushed like a virgin when she saw the paper on her sole.

I wanted to make her come from that moment. Not just come. I wanted her lost in such pleasure that mascara would streak across her china-white cheek.

"*Amore mio,*" I whispered after I exploded inside her.

"Capo," she groaned. "Fuck."

"Those words." She had been so pure when I'd met her. Innocent, yet mature. Her purity was a choice. Sinful words never left her lips until I demanded them, and every time I touched her, she lost a little more spotlessness and came closer to me. Closer to the animal I was. The only moral choice would have been to leave her, but I couldn't. Not because of guilt, even though I had a little of that. But her pull on me, and mine on her made it impossible for me to leave her, even for her own sake. I never felt so helpless in the destruction of graciousness as I did with my Contessa.

"Destroy me," she said, as if I had to be told.

"You're ruined, *amore.*"

She put her hand on my cheek and put her blue eyes to mine. Was it wrong to want her again? Was it immoral to have a desire that grew with the destruction of the object of it?

"Where were you?" she asked. "I don't even know how long you were gone."

"What's the difference?"

"It was too long."

"I agree."

"You should make peace with Paulie," she said.

How was I supposed to tell her that my old partner would not abide her in my life? He'd been very clear about that. As much as I loved Paulie like a brother, I couldn't choose him. The last time I'd thrown Theresa from my life, my future had blinked out like an old bulb.

"I can't," I said. "That's over."

"But, Antonio—"

I put my finger on her lips. "What did you do today?"

"Nothing. I can't leave here."

"Yes, you can, but Otto has to go with you."

"Shouldn't he be working with you? Whatever it is you're doing. Which you won't tell me."

"My most trusted man is with you. As he should be. And if he's not around, you call me, and I'll find someone for you."

She sighed and looked past me to the ceiling. I'd been with many women in my life. I'd cared for some of them and loved only one before Theresa. She was the first who seemed so contented and discontented at the same time.

"You can go shopping," I said. I almost offered her money, but the last time I'd done that, she'd laughed at me. Her reaction to my suggestion wasn't much better.

"Shopping?" She turned her eyes back to me. "Are you joking?" The foul-mouthed girl who begged me to fuck her was gone. She was back to her haughty self. I wanted to fuck the arrogance right out of her, rip away the coating of innocence and take her to the dirty, sexy core again, because it was mine. Only mine.

"Get something nice for me," I said.

"Antonio." She put her thumb on my lip. "I need something to *do*. I need a *life*."

"I can stay the night."

She sighed again. There was something I wasn't getting. Some key to a door I couldn't find. She wasn't fitting into my world. She had nothing to do, and she didn't need me for anything, not support, not money. Nothing I was taught to give a woman was right for Theresa.

She got up, clothed only in her poise. "Someone's going to notice when I'm not around, and when they do, they're going to tell someone else. And before you know it, you're going to see my face on the news, and you're going to wonder what the hell happened. So for your own good, Antonio, I'm telling you: tomorrow I'm leaving, and you're not going to stop me."

She spun on her heel and didn't look back on her way to the bathroom.

We weren't going to last, not as a couple. Not as lovers or sinners. She loved me. I owned her. Her heart was branded with my name. But she'd loved before, and she'd survived. She'd leave me as a matter of practicality.

I avoided death and imprisonment. I protected my territory and my partnerships as a matter of honor and business. But I didn't fear losing those things. I'd had nothing in life, and having nothing again brought no fear.

When she walked to the bathroom without looking back at me, though, I felt fear.

She was my second chance to be whole and clean, and to have a life I'd failed at.

I wasn't losing her.

But I was.

If I kept her under lock and key, I'd lose her. If I tried to keep her too safe, she'd evade me. If I worked too hard to keep her away from my business, she'd want to know more. She was right; she needed a life. I was going to have to provide her with one.

chapter 3.

THERESA

I think he bruised me. Or, more likely, I bruised myself on him. I was going to ache the next day, but if he wanted my body any time between now and then, I'd give it to him.

I leaned into the mirror. The sensitive skin of my neck was reddened and raw where his scruff had abraded me. It didn't matter. It wasn't as though anyone was going to see me anyway.

He came in quietly, no slammed-open door or yelling or grabbing. He just stepped in as if he had every right to.

He took my shoulders. The hands that had hurt were so gentle now, exerting just enough pressure to pull me back and kiss my shoulder. His lips curved themselves to the slopes of my body as if they'd been constructed for my pleasure alone.

"Contessa," he whispered, "I want to ask you something."

"Yes?"

"What do you want?" he asked.

"I don't know. You. I want you. But I don't know how to have you."

"What if you don't have me? What if you're had? You leave it to me, and I'll take care of you."

"Antonio, we talked about this. I have money. I couldn't give it all away in this lifetime."

"I don't mean money."

In the mirror, he considered my shoulder, and brushed the curve of my arm with his thumb like a lit fuse slowly burning.

"What do you mean, then?"

"I mean your safety," he said. "Give me your safety. Abandon any idea you can take care of yourself."

I turned to face him, and he pressed me against the vanity. "But I can take care of myself."

"No." He held a finger up. "You can pay for things. You can manage a political campaign. You can walk into any room and talk to anyone. In your world, you are the Contessa. In my world, you are helpless."

"So, what are you going to do? Send me out in a suit of armor?"

"Don't tempt me." He gave a smirk, and I loved and feared it at the same time.

"Antonio, really, what are the odds Paulie is going to do something stupid to me to win this battle with you? I come from a very large, notorious family. I was engaged to the District Attorney. I'm not trying to throw that in your face; what I'm trying to say is—"

"You're not untouchable."

"I'm not saying I'm untouchable. I'm saying messing with me would be crazy. Suicidal. I'm not only protected by you; I'm protected by the world. It's just who I am. Honestly, my disappearing into this apartment for too long is going to cause more of a problem."

"How?" His eyebrows arched like landmarks, and he looked as if I'd just told him Santa Claus was at the door.

"There are places I go and people I see. Even if I have no life that you can see, someone is going to notice I'm not picking up the phone or taking lunches at Montana's. I'm not saying it's easy to prove an absence, but someone's going to connect that with you and me at Catholic Charities. Someone ambitious and smarter than me."

"Not too many of those around," he said.

"Well, thank you. But the facts remain: I need to be let go without a fuss from you. And soon." I poked his chest. He pulled my arm up by the wrist and put it around his waist. "You said you were going to leave the world. Under *l'uovo*. You said you were getting out. Give Paulie your business and come with me."

"You need to watch more movies," he said.

"Believe me, I've seen plenty."

"Then you know I can't just divide my business and walk away. Even with everything the movies get wrong, they get that part right. And with everything the

FBI thinks they understand, they get that one thing right: I can't just walk away. I can't surrender in the middle of a fight."

"Why not, if you have no more skin in the game?" I said. "Why wouldn't they just let you go?"

"Imagine this. I act like a reasonable man. I divide everything and walk away. I promise you, I'd be a dead man as soon as I turned my back. And you ask why. Why? It's because I have information. I've done things."

I started to ask what, but his expression shushed me.

"Without my family to protect me, I'll be picked up by your ex and questioned. Accused. I can either talk or not talk. If I don't talk, I go to jail, where I'll be murdered to keep me from talking. Or I'll talk, and I can choose between a witness protection program, where you can't join me because of who you are and how well-known your family is. Or I can be murdered in jail for talking."

"What if I made a deal with Daniel to leave you alone?"

He held a finger up in my face, jaw clenched. "Do not—"

I took his wrist and kissed the inside, on the rough, blue tattoo of Mount Vesuvius. I'd asked him if it had hurt to have it burned into such a sensitive area, and he'd laughed and said he practically slept through it.

"If you made peace with Paulie, you wouldn't have to worry about him killing me."

He pressed my hands together between us. "It's been quiet these few days. Zo is working on rebuilding the shop. The Sicilians, Donna Maria and all of them, have stopped complaining that the Neapolitans are fighting. I'm just starting to breathe."

"Can I speak my mind?" I said.

"How can you not?"

"I don't trust her patience. When a political opponent doesn't respond to an attack or an offer, he's not just sitting there waiting for something to happen; he's gathering ammunition. The worst thing you can do is give him time to arm himself."

He pressed our hands together pensively then kissed my fingertips. "You have a devil of a mind, Contessa."

"What are you going to do about it, Capo?"

He stared down at our pressed hands as if considering something. "There is something distracting the Sicilians. A wedding."

"They can't plan a wedding and run a business at the same time?" I said.

"Not their wedding. It's a wedding between a Neapolitan family, the Bortolusis, and a rival Sicilian family, the Leis. This doesn't happen often. Sicilian mafias have a tower of payoffs. Don, boss, underboss, capo, on and on. I'm Neapolitan camorra. We're smaller. We don't step on each other. We don't have all these people to answer to, just the capo then Napoli if something goes bad."

"Like with you and Paulie?"

"Like that," he said. "But we don't marry across organizations. Sicilians and Neapolitans don't have a matching structure. It's more trouble then it's worth. So it's just not done. Because marriage is for love when possible, but for business, when necessary."

"And this one is business?"

"Yes. And it's a problem, a big problem, because it makes them too powerful, now. And Donna Maria Carloni needs to answer it or get crushed. She has a granddaughter, raised in Sicily, a good match for a nice Neapolitan boy."

"Do not even tell me you're short-listed."

He smiled. "They have someone. Nice boy. Little *stupido*, but he'll do for her."

"And what's your job in all this?"

"My job is to fuck you until the neighbors think I'm murdering you."

I kissed his cheek, his chin, his lips. He was erect in less than a minute, and when he carried me to the bedroom, I fell into a suit of armor.

chapter 4.

ANTONIO

I'd gotten used to helicopters. I'd seen them in Napoli as they blasted along the coast, taking tourists along the beach or finding lost boats. But helicopters—Los Angeles style, with their low circles over a block or house—were a different experience.

The first time I'd been exposed to the loud *thup-thup-thup,* I'd been near LAX, having just gotten off the plane in order to do the dirty business of avenging my sister's rape with certain death.

"It's called a double-double," Paulie said. I didn't know him yet. He was just the guy who'd met me at the airport and driven me to a restaurant for a hamburger.

"It's huge." I held the humungous thing in one hand and a soda, which was also too big, in the other. In Napoli, we didn't eat like that until the sun set.

We stood in the parking lot because there were no seats, and Paulie said it would be more private anyway. He leaned against the red Ferrari and bit into his burger. Sauce dripped down his chin, and he caught it with a napkin. "It's good. Try it."

As soon as I lifted the sandwich, the helicopter came into range. I looked up then back to Paulie.

"Don't worry about it," he said. "Not us."

I looked up again. The helicopter turned in circles over the skies.

"It's three hundred meters away," I said.

"Is that far or near? What the fuck is that?"

"Close. And low. No one cares?"

"Would you eat the thing? Jesus. I'll eat it if you don't want it."

I was hungry. I put my soda in the tray that sat on the hood of the car, and bit down.

"It's good," I said, trying to ignore the low-flying helicopter with the letters LAPD painted across it.

"*Molto bene*? Right?"

"Don't."

"Don't what?" he said.

"Speak Italian. Ever again, please. It's like gears grinding."

"Fuck you, dago motherfucker."

"*Porci Americano*."

"Oink oink, asshole," he said with a mouth full of food.

I replied, but I've forgotten what I said, and the sound of the helicopter drowned me out anyway. But in the past weeks, the sound of helicopters has reminded me of Paulie and of what had happened to our friendship because of a woman.

"What do you want to eat?" I asked, when the sound of traffic helicopters woke Theresa. "I'll have Zia bring it."

She rolled onto her stomach, tucking her hands under her thighs. "She hates me."

"She doesn't hate you."

"She won't look me in the eye."

"She doesn't trust Irish Catholics. It's not personal." I drew my hand over her ass, which was snowy and pure. She didn't fidget in her nudity, didn't try to cover herself or play at modesty. Not with me.

"I want to see Katrina," she said. "She's been calling."

The movie director, Katrina Ip, had started the trouble in the first place. Theresa was financing her movie. I supported her talking to Katrina, just not as long as Paulie was acting crazy. "Not yet," I said. "Soon."

She rolled over and got out of the bed. I grabbed her by the wrist. I think I had her more firmly than I'd intended, because she tried to yank away and couldn't.

"This is not a joke," I said. "This is not a competition for who has control over you."

She growled. The guttural sound of it stiffened my dick. I pulled her harder. "The first time I lost a woman I loved, it was easy to get my vengeance, but it didn't bring her back. Nothing brought her back. The second time, when my sister was hurt, they were ready for me. I did what I had to do, but now the consequence is that

I can't go home. If anything happens to you, the consequence will be my death. I'm ready to die if anyone takes you. But they won't kill or hurt you because I was lazy or because you were proving some point about your independence."

"You can't sustain this, Capo."

"I can. As long as Paulie sets himself against me, you're a target."

She softened, moving into me, so I didn't have to grip her so hard. "And the next enemy? Who is it going to be? If you win with Paulie, that only sets you up for the next challenge. I can't live like this."

She balled her fists in frustration. I pitied her. She hadn't been born into this. She didn't understand it.

"Let me ask you a question," I said. "You have a, shall we say, infamous family. You aren't unknown."

"I've worked my whole life to be normal."

"Good job. You've been shopping recently?"

"Before you holed me up?" she asked.

"Yes."

"I went to Rodeo on—"

"To the grocery store. To buy towels. Sheets. Soap. Have you ever washed a dish?"

"Yes, I have," she said. "But I see your point. Even if it's irrelevant."

I pulled her onto the bed and wrapped my arms around her. "Tell me about that scar on your lip, and tell me you haven't always been protected."

She rested her head on my chest and didn't say anything. I thought she'd fallen asleep. I was considering how to get out from under her, so I could do what I had to do for the day, when she spoke.

"We rented a cabin every year, up by Santa Barbara. It was a campground, but really, more of a pretend-rustic resort. And there was this kid who lived in the area. He was older than me. I think I was seven when we first met, and he was eleven or twelve. He lived in an RV with his mother, and they just had it arranged so he could go to the schools up there. But, every year I found him by this narrow little river at the edge of the campsite. I was the youngest girl of seven, and I was so sick of my family. My mom just talked to the other moms and drank wine. And my dad talked business with his friends. So boring. And this guy? He was wild. We climbed trees and went past every fence we were supposed to stay behind. I think I was the kid sister he always wanted. Or maybe not. Because…"

She stopped herself to sigh, wiggling around until she was looking up at me. "I was thirteen, and he was older. We met in the same place, the Thursday of Labor Day weekend. After dinner, same as always. It was different. I was different. We sat on our rock and talked for a while. He showed me his high-school ring, and then he kissed me. You know, I didn't think about how young I was. I just thought I liked him. And maybe I loved him. Or, maybe I just wanted to. But, God, I never told anyone this before."

"You can stop."

"He put his fingers in me. I came right there. I just about died. And he… he came, too, all over my shirt. I never even touched him, which I didn't know could happen. And it was such a mess, and I was so surprised that I laughed. I didn't mean anything by it. It was nerves, and it was funny. But I must have hurt his feelings because he hit me, and his ring caught my lip. There was blood everywhere. And that's the scar right here. I told my dad I fell, and he didn't say a word the whole way to the doctor. Got two stitches. When I got back to the cabin, I realized I had cum all over my shirt, in front of my dad and everything."

She laughed to herself, a soft chuckle that sounded like nerves. I touched the scar. You could barely see it unless you were the type of man who looked for damage.

"What happened to the boy?"

She rolled over until she faced the ceiling. "They found his body at the bottom of the gulch the next morning. The rocks can be really slippery. I slept in until lunch because of the pills the doctor gave me. If I'd gotten up, who knows what would have happened?"

"What do you think would have happened?"

She stared out the window then back to me. "I would have found him. But I was spared that. Same as I've been spared everything."

chapter 5.

THERESA

I'd told Daniel that story, up to the kid at the bottom of the gulch, but I'd never mentioned the silent car ride, or the sticky adolescent semen all over my shirt. I had never felt safe telling him. Daniel had a suspicious mind, same as Antonio, but he was the DA, and ambitious, and there was no statute of limitations on murder.

From my window perch, I watched Antonio walk out of the building and toward the bench where Otto sat. Antonio had entered the camorra to avenge his wife. Then he came to Los Angeles to avenge his sister, and as much as he wanted me safe, and as much as I wanted to live, I didn't want to be the reason for his vengeance. I could ruin his life while I lived, but in dying, I could destroy his soul, so I stayed. For the time being.

Daniel was on television again, talking, talking, talking. I could count his bullet points off on my fingers, and they'd gotten tighter and meaner, undoubtedly due to Clarice's influence. There was a distinct lean away from previous talk of generic crime fighting and more emphasis on organized crime. Antonio and I had gotten out of the yellow house, *l'uovo,* with whatever the DA had needed before they got there with his warrant. That fact burned Daniel. He'd planned everything to a T, except the traffic caused by the arson of Antonio's shop and me shutting off my phone.

There would come a day when near misses weren't going to sit well with Daniel anymore. He wasn't biting his nails or flipping his hair back, but his ambition was challenged, and there was something a little feral about him. No one liked looking foolish. No one liked failing. But Daniel played a high-stakes game, and the more he tried to win, the more I felt like a cornered chess piece.

chapter 6.

ANTONIO

Zo waited in the driver's seat of my car, under the building's sign, which read *The Afidnes Tower* in big gold Grecian letters.

"Hey," Zo said as he ripped into a sandwich. "You want some?"

"No. Where's Otto?"

"He went to feel up his wife eighty percent worth." He laughed at his joke.

"You need a break?" I said.

"Me? Nah. We got a bunch of permits cleared for the shop. Had to do a little song and dance, but fuck, I feel like, you know, useful when I'm building shit. Or you know, when I'm telling a bunch of other guys what to build. And I want the shop up and running so that *stronzo* sees it and sees it good."

"All right, all right. Easy." I slapped his back. "Go take care of it."

"You got it." Zo gave me a thumbs-up and got out of my car. I took his place and headed for a little empty storefront on the east side.

My cold feelings toward Paulie surprised me. There wasn't a woman alive who had meant as much to me as Paulie had. Maybe not even a human being. I had no brothers, and my father had been a shade of a man until I walked into his coffee shop at eleven years old to settle a dispute.

But Paulie, though a *camorrista* deeply connected to the Carloni family through a couple of generations of business ties, had earned my trust in the first few minutes at the airport.

I'd been photographed on the Italy side like a criminal, but once I'd arrived in Los Angeles, I was a dot in a newspaper photo. I stood a second too long under the arch of the international terminal, overwhelmed by the size, the multicolored crowd, and the expanse of space and light. The public address system went on and on about loading and unloading, lines, flight times, gates. I smiled through security, had my bag inspected at customs, and got taken aside briefly for questioning. It was easy on the Los Angeles side.

I went outside to noise and smog that wasn't much worse than Napoli, which was urban to the teeth at the center and more and more pastoral the closer you got to Vesuvio.

Paulie stood by a chrome pillar that was stained with an old spray of blackened soda. He wore skinny jeans, white shoes, and Ray Bans, which he flipped up when he saw me.

"You Racossi?" he asked in shitty Italian.

"Spinelli," I replied, nervous about my just-passable English. I felt vulnerable without a weapon, and he must have felt like that, too. As far as I knew, it was impossible to get a gun into the airport, even for people with connections.

"Donna Carloni wants to talk to you," he said.

"I'm not here to get involved. I'm here to finish some business and go home."

I dragged my bag and walked away. He caught up, crossing the street to the cabs with me.

"I don't think you can refuse." A bus stopped near us, beeping when it kneeled, the driver shouting over an intercom for passengers to exit through the back. The noise was enormous, and the heat was oppressive.

"I don't take orders from Sicilians." I didn't know if that came off right in English. In the end, it was Paulie who helped me understand the nuances of the language. But on that day, I could only use the words I knew.

"You need her say-so to finish this business you got, or she's going to get in your way. And let's face it, you don't know up from down. If she offers you help, you oughta take it." He stepped in front of me. "She sent me because I'm *camorrista*. Like you."

"There's enough off-the-boot in your blood. I can see it."

"Jesus, man." He showed me the inside of his left wrist, where a tattoo of a volcano was drawn. The high peak was on the left. I took his wrist and pulled the skin. It wasn't pen. It was real. I didn't want to trust it. Anybody can get a tattoo.

"This is Vesuvio from the Pompeii side," I said, dropping his hand. I pulled up my left sleeve and held out my wrist, where the active side was drawn on the right.

"I know, man. Dude got it from a book. What do you want me to tell you? Nobody's actually been to fucking Naples."

"No," I poked his chest. "Nobody has been to Pompeii." I walked off, heading for what looked like a taxi stand.

"What are you going to do?" he said, chasing me. "Walk up and down Sunset, showing a mug shot? You're gonna get pegged for a narc by the gangs and for a dago criminal by the cops before your tourist visa's even up."

"I have leads."

"Not as good as mine. Come on. I know what they did to your sister. And I know why." He stepped in front of me and dropped his voice. "I'm going to be honest. They got a big chunk of the east side, and I want it. Give me a chance to do business and avenge a lady at the same time."

Something about the guy's straightforwardness appealed to me, and the fact that he'd known I'd be there intrigued me.

"I see," I said. "My father told Donna Maria I was coming."

"I can't say whether or not there was a phone conversation last night. I got nothing. 'Cause, you know, on the surface, he don't even agree with you being here. On the surface, he wants it taken care of on the Naples side, by Neapolitans. By him. Not you. You're a *consigliere*, dude. You don't get to do vendettas."

"But you do."

He shrugged, confirming it with the gesture.

"And a contract gets you made," I said.

He gave another gesture with a bobbing head that seemed affirmative.

"If I go with you," I said, "that doesn't mean I'm agreeing to anything."

He smiled. "You ever had an In-'n-Out burger?"

"*Scusa?*" I didn't know if he was propositioning me, or what.

"A burger. You hungry?"

"Yes. I am."

"Let's go then," he said. "You're gonna love it here."

I never did. But I paid my debts, and the price of allowing the vendetta to take place was two years of my life in the service of a Sicilian. It was worth it.

chapter 7.

THERESA

Eventually, I did need to leave the apartment. I picked up some things from the loft—cash, valuables, toiletries, even Daniel's engagement ring—then went shopping on Rodeo, which was a complete waste of time, even after I'd dropped a few grand. I ignored a call from Katrina and my eleventh text from Margie. I wasn't interested in explaining myself to anyone, since I couldn't even explain myself to myself.

Otto took me back to the *Afidnes Tower.* I stood there, waiting for an approved activity. Or a signal that I could move back home safely. Would Antonio allow tonight to pass without crawling between the sheets with me?

As Otto and I waited for the elevator, I texted Antonio.

> —*I'm back from lunch. I'm thinking of jumping out the window—*

—Let me jump you first—

—Tonight?—

*—I have something to show you
first—*

I was formulating a snappy retort, something along the lines of a grownup show-and-tell, with nudity, when Otto opened the door to the apartment. I was shoved back so hard the wind went out of me.

I never realized how big Otto was until I tried to see past him and couldn't. His shoulders turned in, as if his arms were in front of him. The fact that I knew he was pointing a gun said a lot about what I'd been through.

"It's all right," said a man's voice on the other side of Otto's bulk. "We're friends."

"Like hell," said Otto.

"Ask her," came a woman's voice. "Sometime before you crush her against the wall."

"Margie!" I pushed past Otto to get to my sister.

"You know these people?" Otto asked as I hugged Margie. I didn't know who the man was. He was mid to late thirties, maybe, or late twenties with a ton of extra experience that aged him ten years. He had dark hair and light-brown eyes, but he wasn't Italian. And even though he wore a pinkie ring, he didn't look mob. Not that it meant anything because mob or not, he and Otto had guns leveled at each other as if they meant to shoot first and deal with the handcuffs later.

Margie had her red hair up in a chignon, and she wore a snappy business suit as if she'd cancelled a meeting to break into my fake apartment.

I left Margie's arms and stood between the two guns. "Guys, really?"

"Who are you?" Otto asked.

"Will Santon."

"He's with me," Margie said. "That's all you need to know."

"And you?" he asked Margie.

"She's my sister." I put my hand on Otto's wrist. "They're okay." I looked him in the eye, transmitting sincerity and seriousness, until he lowered the weapon.

"*Mi dispiace*" he said to Margie. He shot Will a dirty look before stepping out the door. I clicked it behind him, and before I could let Margie know that Antonio would likely interrupt us in a few minutes, she reached behind me and locked the door.

"What is wrong with you?" I asked.

"You should try answering your phone."

"I was busy."

"Doing what?"

Will interjected as he removed files from a briefcase, "Hanging around Alberto Mongelluzo, apparently."

"His name's Otto."

"No it's not. Otto's the Italian word for eight." He holds up his pinkies. "You should ask him how he lost these. It wasn't a golfing accident."

"Who are you, again?" I asked.

Margie sat in my chair. "Mr. Santon freelances for my firm, and today, he's doing me a favor."

"That's a fucking answer?" I said.

"Correct use of the word fuck. Well done."

"Don't be a bitch. And no clever quips. Just answer."

She sighed. "I think I liked you better when you acted like a lady. But all right; before you tear my face off, Will works for me. He finds things out, does research, and kidnaps my sisters when necessary. He's a good guy. You should be nice to him."

"Antonio's going to show up about five minutes after he finds out you're here."

"That's the problem, isn't it?"

"I'm making tea. Do you want any? Or is it just bust in and run?"

"Coffee," Margie said.

"Dark and bitter, I presume?" I stormed into the kitchen before she had a chance to answer.

Why did she make me feel like a prepubescent? Was it because she was more of a mother to me than my actual mother, who popped designer pills between emotional outbursts? Margie had earned the mother role by giving me affection and gaining my trust where no one else had, but her methods were drastic and overbearing, and apparently included breaking and entering.

"You broke into this apartment because you don't like who I'm sleeping with?"

"'Don't like' is mild. Very Old Theresa. New Theresa would say something more colorful. So I'll tell you this. The guy you're fucking terrifies me, and I'm just going to spoon-feed you some sense before Daddy gets wind of it."

A phone rang in the other room. I peeked in, wondering if it was Antonio. Santon placed piles of files on the coffee table and answered his phone. Margie dialed hers. I heard everything while I slapped the pieces of the coffee maker together.

"Good evening to you too, little brother." She turned to look into the kitchen. I ducked away. "You have Will Santon's team flying to Vancouver to watch Kevin Wainwright?"

Margie, single at forty-seven, had never been in love as far as I knew. She'd been a model of sharp, dirty, cut-and-dried sense; even her tone over the phone to our brother was tidy and utilitarian. As if love made sense. Love didn't stay on budget or check to see if the ledger balanced. Love didn't care if all things were equal. Love bathed the books in red, shredded documents, spent more than it brought in one month and paid too much income tax the next.

When I came in with cream and sugar, I heard Jonathan's voice, made tinny though the phone as he shouted, "Physically and irrevocably hurt."

"You know, Jonny," Margie said, "I don't mind you getting paranoid and crazy, but you're doing it on my dime."

Jonathan growled something, and I went back into the kitchen.

"Now you're getting nasty," said Margie pointedly, yet without an ounce of upset in her voice. "I gotta pull him, Jonny. I'm sorry."

She hung up just as I came back with the coffee. "I just lied for you."

"You want a medal?"

"I'd like some appreciation."

"For coming into my apartment uninvited? Because I didn't answer your texts in the right amount of time? Because you don't approve of the man I love?"

"Oh, it's love now. Great." She tossed her phone on the coffee table and grabbed a cup. "I've never seen anyone make a good decision for love."

"Love is its own decision," Will cut in. "It chooses you."

"Thanks, Delta," Margie said. "You can engrave that on your headstone." She turned back to me. "You already made it clear you wanted nothing to do with what I had to say. I stopped caring what you wanted when Dad asked if you were really with that guy from the Catholic Charities thing."

"What did you tell him?" I said.

"I laughed. But he knew I was evading." She snapped open a briefcase and swung it over to Will. It was his, and she was hurrying him.

"He can't control who we're with," I said.

"He does like to try."

"And you?" I glanced at Will, then back to Margie. "What is it you're trying to do?"

Will cut in. "We're educating you." He removed a file and opened it on the coffee table.

Antonio. Even his mug shot made me tingle: the curl of his smirk, the jaw set in anger, the tousled black hair. He was younger in the photo and had a reckless edge. His mouth was shaped for a different language, and the lines around his eyes were somehow unset, reversible. He watched me from a wallet-sized rectangle stapled to a document that told me what had been implied but never stated.

"Antonio Spinelli is the bastard son of Benito Racossi." Will put his elbows on his knees, the angle of the sun cutting his face into dark and light sides. "By the time he found out who his father was, he'd already made a name for himself as a petty criminal and pickpocket. He went to his father to settle a dispute between himself and another thief who'd stolen a shipment of his bootleg cigarettes. He was eleven. A prodigy, even by Neapolitan standards."

"Look at you." Margie, arms crossed, leaned back in the chair. "You got a face like a brick wall. You don't want to hear it, because you already decided you don't care. This mug shot, it's Interpol's. He was accused of killing the men who killed his wife."

This story wasn't new or shocking, though I guess it should have been. I guess if anyone else heard their lover had murdered someone, they'd be upset. But I wasn't just anyone. I was a savage.

"She took a car bomb that was meant for him," Will said. "He was visiting a client in a neighboring town. His business partner drove, which saved

Spinelli's life and ended his wife's. He killed the two
guys allegedly responsible."

"And?" I flipped through the file, moving quickly
past the photos of the bodies of the men who'd killed
his wife. Allegedly killed. "It's just a theory. Do you
want me to say, 'Oh, darling, welcome home, let me
take your coat, what exactly happened with your
wife?'"

"You could start by asking about the real-estate-
assessment racket," Will said. "Go on to the money
laundering, the car insurance fraud out of his shop, the
sideline in tax-free cigarettes, and the occasional truck
hijack on the 60 freeway."

"If that's not enough to make you ill," Margie said,
"I don't know why you even need a car-bombed
spouse."

It didn't make me ill. Not a bit. It made me curious
and hungry. And a little turned on. I was fascinated not
by the wife but by the web of underground criminal
activity and the way he'd mastered it. He'd turned East
Los Angeles into his own marionette theater.

I hid my excitement behind a cold stare and a
raised chin. As if she saw right through me, Margie got
out of her chair and looked down at me. "I'm trying to
say things so you hear them. I love you. I want to
protect you. How has he protected you?"

"Maybe it's time everyone stopped trying to
protect me." I stood up. I'd heard enough facts I
already knew and the rest was conjecture. "Will needs
to go back to doing whatever he was doing for
Jonathan, because there's nothing here to fix."

I started to leave. Margie took my shoulder. "Please, Theresa. It's going to get worse, and you're going to be a target."

"How could it be worse?"

"There's a wedding," Will said, gathering his papers and files.

"I know all about it."

"It's a serious imbalance. No one knows how it's going to be rectified, but it won't be bloodless. All I have to say is Spinelli will have to get involved. His life isn't his own. Never was."

"Speak clearly, Mr. Santon. Tell me what you mean. You didn't come all this way to make insinuations."

His mouth curled into a knowing grin. He was a nice-looking man with brown eyes and scruffy black hair he'd tamed into something conservative and nondescript. "You really are all cut from the same cloth," he said warmly.

"Enough, Delta," Margie cut in. "Get to the point."

He cleared his throat and sat back. "To correct the imbalance, Donna Maria Carloni is going to have to have a granddaughter marry into a nice Neapolitan family with ties to the old country. The most likely candidate is a young lady named Irene. She's just been flown in from Sicily, where she was educated in the old way. She is unsullied, if you will."

It was funny, what came to mind. Will was describing a young woman educated in a particular way to achieve a certain goal and groomed in behavior and speech, much the way I'd been.

"Well," I said. "I hope she likes it here. If she can stay a virgin for fifteen minutes, I salute her."

"Oh, she'll stay a virgin," Margie said. "Because the Neapolitan who was supposed to marry her has disappeared."

"The *stupido*?"

"And his girlfriend." Will handed me a picture of a nice-looking couple on the beach. He was dark-haired and bulky, smiling. She was cute as soda pop, mousy blond and cap toothed.

"Theresa," Margie said softly. "Get out while you can. It's chaos."

"You were there when the thing happened with Daniel. You saw me. You saw what I went through. You want that again?"

"I'll take it over a funeral."

"I can't; it's too late. I love him, and whatever he faces, I face with him."

"You might face it without him. He's part of a world you don't understand; he'll cut you out, and you won't even know what hit you."

"You don't know anything," I growled. "You're so closed off. You're so scared. You run every piece of information through your worry filter, and nothing gets through unscathed. You calculate everything that can go wrong, and when you're done doing it for yourself, you do it for the rest of us. I think you were happiest when I was alone and not taking any risks. You need to stop. You need to let me try and be happy."

"I can offer this," Will interrupted. "I know you won't take protection from the authorities because of

Daniel. But I can offer it to you separate from that. I have contacts in the military who can keep you safe from Paulie Patalano, Antonio Spinelli, Donna Maria. All of them."

"I don't even know you."

"It's through me," Margie said. "Limited-time offer."

"Thanks for the offer, Margie," I said, "but I have mistakes to make."

As if summoned by the word "mistake," the latch turned, and Antonio walked in as if he owned the place. A second passed, or a fraction of one, during which all parties assessed the imminent threat of danger. Antonio was armed, as was Will; I knew that much. If either of them was worth his salt, he would smell it on the other.

"*Buongiorno*," Antonio said with a smile. The three of us stood. I went to him, kissing each cheek. He put his hand on the small of my back.

"Antonio, have you met my sister, Margie?"

"I haven't," he said, smiling to her and offering his hand. They shook.

"Nice to meet you," she said. "This is my friend Will Santon." They shook hands, as well. The distrust in the room was palpable, multiplying exponentially, like compound interest on a bad loan.

"Tea? Coffee?" I offered, half joking.

"A butter knife for the tension, please," Margie said.

"Something serrated might help?" Antonio offered.

"You'd know, apparently."

"Margie!"

"I don't like niceties," Margie said. "They bore me."

"Of course, then." Antonio spoke the words with one hand extended, as if offering peace, and the other firmly planted at the base of my neck. "Let's skip all that. How can I help you?"

"You can let my sister answer her calls."

"Your sister does what I ask her to because she knows what's best for her."

The conversation was going nowhere in a big hurry. If I knew anything about Margie, her intention had been to leave the apartment with me, and she wasn't walking out any other way. If I knew anything about Antonio, she was going to have to walk over a dead body to do it. So, either the unstoppable force and the immovable object were going to have a meet up, or I was going to step in between them.

"I can pick up my phone any time, Margaret. But I don't want to. I'm sorry; I wasn't trying to worry you or stress you out. But you really have to step back and trust that if I'm not answering the phone, I'm busy. I want you to consider that no news is good news." She started to say something, and I held my hand up. "I'm not in a bit of danger. Boredom is my biggest problem right now. Antonio," I said, turning to him, "you tell my sister you're bossing me around, and she's going to get a SWAT team in here. Personally, I don't need the aggravation."

"I'm sorry, then," he said, facing Margie. "Of course, she's a grown woman, in America."

I held my hand out to Will. "Mr. Santon, thanks for coming. I appreciate your candor. I hope we never meet again."

"Feeling's mutual," he said as we shook on it.

I separated from Antonio and went to the door with a cold spot at the back of my neck where his hand had been. I opened it. Otto was waiting in the hallway.

"I promise I will pick up my phone from now on, as long as you don't unleash a stream of neuroses on me."

Margie brushed her skirt down and composed herself, which meant, in Drazen parlance, that she was about to unleash a torrent of The Truth According To Margaret, and nothing could stop her, not a word, gesture, or forward tackle.

"I'm fine with being dismissed like a child, and I'm fine with you not taking my advice. I can walk out of here without a problem. But when the last asshole did things I don't even want to talk about, I was the first one you called. And I was the one who stood by you for the whole thing." She slashed the air with the flat of her hand, the gesture filling in for words like bawling, suicidal depression, the inability to move, long bouts of self-doubt, reproach, and loathing. She'd been with me for every minute of it, and with that karate chop, I relived it.

"And I want you to know," she continued without pausing, though my brain had hitched, "that the next time you call me because you're in over your head, and you can't handle what's happening, I will pick up the phone, and I'll be there for you again. And I won't even say 'I told you so.'"

"Thank you," I said, because there was nothing else in my vocabulary for that speech. She tilted her head down and left, with Will close at her heels. He and Antonio nodded to each other. I shut the door softly then pressed my back to it.

Antonio's face betrayed nothing but perfection. I felt cornered by his beauty, soothed to inaction. I slid away so I could think.

"We have to talk," I said. "And you're keeping your pants on for the entire thing."

"You're going to talk," he said, holding up a finger and stepping so close our bodies shared the same heat. "And I'm going to keep my pants on."

He leaned forward until I took a step backward, and in the second of slight imbalance, he grabbed my shoulders, directing me into the chair behind me. I didn't know what to ask first. He looked down at me with a fully visible erection, and the whole pants-on rule seemed really badly thought out. "You're going to take these pants off. Then you're going to spread your legs so I can see everything, and you're going to tell me what they said to you."

"Why do you need me vulnerable to hear this? Don't you trust me?"

"I don't need you vulnerable," he said, leaning down and hooking his fingers in my waistband. "I need you accessible."

"I'm going to tell you everything. You know that already."

"Then it's only right you should enjoy it."

He yanked my pants down. They were loose, silk things and came off easily, taking my underpants with them. I tried to get up just to prove a point, but he pushed me against the chair. "Spread your legs, Contessa."

I didn't. He pushed me down with his right hand and took my knee in the other, wrapping his fingers around it easily and yanking it to the side. I gasped as the rush of fluids drenched me. He slid his hand down my chest and kneeled in front of me.

"Your sister is an honest woman," he said, kissing my mound and working his way down. "So it's not important what she said, only what she thinks."

His tongue, honed to a point, slid down, parting my skin. The invasion was delicate and sweet, warm on warm, wet to wet, and I melted into the chair.

"I don't care about any of it, Antonio."

"Really?" He kissed my clit, folding his lips around it, closing them, tightening, sucking just enough, and releasing. "Tell me what you don't care about."

"You want a list?"

He licked me harder in response, and I pushed myself into his mouth, running my fingers through his black hair. He awakened a galaxy of burning stars that turned in the universe between my legs.

"She thinks you're a killer, a criminal. Money laundering, insurance fraud, oh, God, just like that. Keep doing that thing." He slid a finger into me and rotated it, not saying a word, but with his eyes, he told me to continue.

"You're going to hurt me," I gasped as his tongue swirled. "She's afraid for me." The burning points of heat and light coalesced into a bright center, and when he moaned, his mouth vibrated against me. I wanted to tell him more, but I couldn't when the galaxy spun into itself and exploded, my orgasm a black hole of wordless ecstasy.

When I could speak, I said, "Now. Take me now."

But he was already there, pants down, glorious cock stretching me open, his weight on me the comfort and security I needed. The protection Margie thought I wasn't getting was him and me together: his thumb in my mouth, his dick owning me, his control and dominance frightening, deadly, and indispensable.

He came with a grunt, and I was right behind him, screaming his name again, tightening my legs around him, bucking as he held me still.

Through the post-orgasmic haze, I could barely hear his soft words in a musical language or feel the light kisses he laid on my cheek and neck.

"Capo," I whispered.

"Contessa."

"I wasn't finished."

He picked up his head and looked me in the eyes. "You feel finished."

I laid my hand on his cheek, stroking the short hairs, their resistance pleasing my skin. "I need to finish what I was saying. About Margie."

"You don't have to finish." He sighed and straightened his arms, putting twelve or so inches between us. "She's more or less got a point. I'm bad for you. And you have a point also."

"I do?"

"I think I've been wrong. I think if I keep you here, trouble will find you. So, get out. Go do… I don't know. Find your life."

"Oh, Antonio…" I didn't know whether to assure him that my life was with him or thank him for coming around to giving me space.

"But please, be safe. Can you do that for me? Until Paulie is calm."

"What happened to the *stupido* and his girlfriend?" I asked.

He put his fingers on my lips. "Not now. Just tell me you'll let Otto take you around."

I promised. I'd keep as safe as I could.

chapter 8.

THERESA

Katrina's post-production rental was on the west side in some in-between neighborhood. The low-slung buildings in a three-block radius had been painted yellowish beige and sprinkled with Spanish roof tiles, black soot, and garish signs in three languages.

Otto walked me to the double glass doors that faced into the parking lot.

"Where will you be?" I asked as we passed into the small reception area.

"I have to check it out. Then I'll be right here." With a pinky-less hand, he indicated a leather chair by a plastic plant.

"You can grab a cup of coffee if you want."

He smiled and nodded, but prior experience told me that he wouldn't get himself a cup of anything.

The receptionist, a young Hispanic girl with straight hair down her back, said "Which project?"

"*The Lion In the Sand*?" I said. "I think they're in edit."

She checked her computer. "They have a bay on four."

Otto took me upstairs, and when we left the elevator, I turned to him, saying nothing but giving him a look. He understood and nodded.

"I'll be here." He indicated a bank of couches.

"Thank you."

I went past the double doors alone.

Katrina leaned into the monitor. The overhead lights were dimmed down to nothing, leaving only the four glowing editing-bay monitors to illuminate the trays of half-eaten burgers. The room smelled of men and salty food. Her editor, Robbie, tapped keys. Michael Greenwich's face, all lion and rage, filled the screen.

"This is the best take," Robbie said. He motioned to his assistant. "Rob, call up number four."

Katrina leaned back. "I'll look, but I think you're right. TeeDray, what do you think? You marked four as the best." She tapped my set notes.

"Look at four again. But this is it. I mean, who can tell anything on set?" I shrugged, and Katrina eyed me as if I were lying. She grabbed our Styrofoam boxes and went to the door.

"Let's eat. You look like you could use it."

The light in the hall was blinding on the white walls. Burgundy doors lined the corridor. Each had a little square, meshed window at eye level, and behind them came the sounds of screaming, music, crashes, whispers, and groans. Editors didn't understand moderation of volume, and headphones would have given them a headache after twelve hours of chopping up scenes.

Katrina led me to the lounge at the end of the hall, which consisted of plywood boxes covered in grey industrial carpet that matched the floors. No windows. No tables. Dated movie posters. There was a vending machine that reminded me of Antonio and, in front of it, a brown-splat stain that would never come out, no matter how hard they shampooed.

"What the hell is wrong with you?" Katrina flipped open the Styrofoam box and shoved my well-done burger toward me, pushing it against my thigh. I moved so she would have room to open hers. Her burger would be rare. She liked it squealing as it went down.

It had been a week since I'd seen her. I hadn't answered any texts but had left a voice message when Antonio told me it was safe for her to come home. I believed him, because he knew his business.

"Well?" she said with a mouthful of fries.

"I don't know where to start." My fries looked like a bundle of Jack Straws. I tried to pick one up without disturbing any of the others and failed.

"Throw the first scene out," Katrina said. "Always."

"I'm in love with Antonio."

"That was fast."

"Yeah," I said.

"But?"

I looked up at the walls to think for a second and was hit with a poster for Good Fellas. I laughed to myself. Even in that bland, windowless room, he hung over me. "I understand him. It's weird. There's this connection. I get what he's saying, and I know what keeps him up at night. It sounds crazy, but I know what's in his heart."

"That sounds pretty good."

"It's different. With Daniel, I knew what was in his mind. I knew what he was thinking; I just didn't know what he was feeling. Obviously, or that whole Clarice thing wouldn't have gotten past me." I brought my burger to my lips and bit it. It tasted like every other well-done burger. The texture was grey and leathery. Flat. Boiled dry. Katrina's burger dripped when she bit into it. "With Antonio, I'm alive when he's there. It's chemical. My blood goes crazy."

"Wow."

I shrugged. "Yeah."

"Oh, for Christ's sake, Tee. What's the problem? Speak. You're boring me."

"It's complicated."

She chewed slowly then took a pull of her soda. "I'm waiting."

"How is the edit coming?"

"Fine. I think I got most everything. Michael's in Montana doing a spelunking movie, so if I need pickups, I'm screwed. Why don't you tell me why it's so complicated?"

"It just is."

"Oh, for the love of God. He's in the mob. Just say it."

"Katrina!" I said.

"Please, sister. I wasn't born yesterday. One, he was having you followed by that guy with no pinkies. Two, it's all over the news that shit's going down. Your ex is taking out the flamethrowers and threatening the biggest prosecution since Robert Kennedy in like, the sixties. Which I'd blow off, except I met Antonio and yes, he's hot, but also… he's got a whole connected thing happening. Three, you disappeared in a poof after the wrap party."

"I did not."

"You talk on the phone and don't tell me where you are. Have you even been to the apartment?"

I put my burger down. "Antonio is a businessman. His office was burned down. His partner split and took half his team. He's rebuilding, and I'm there for him."

"Uh-huh. Fine. And what else?"

"What do you mean?"

"You have no job. You're not talking to me." She leaned forward. "A lot of fucking, huh?"

I pulled out a fry and it rubbed against another. Five more shifted in the container. "There is sex." I bent the fry against my tongue and folded it into my mouth. "And it is life altering."

She smiled and raised her eyebrows, delighted for me. I couldn't tell her about my ennui, or the level of protection Antonio felt he needed to build around me. I couldn't tell her that, from the outside, he deserved every indecent name I called him during sex and that it turned me on. How far he would go, his life on the fringes, the unknowns about him, and even his insistence that I bend to the will of an outlaw turned me on. And I feared that, without those hours of languor in between our meetings, the desire for him to dig out the aching filth inside me would disappear. And I needed it. I needed him to treat me like a rag doll while I called him an animal. I needed to see that animal turn pure, to feel him slowly get gentle, to hear his growls subdued into whispers. Thinking about it in that little room, under a Good Fellas poster, melted my legs into a pool of lust.

"Have you considered this might be a rebound thing? From Daniel?"

"Sure," I said. "I've considered it then dismissed it. If rebound things always felt like this, they'd last longer."

My phone dinged.

—downstairs in 10 minutes—

—I'm busy—

I didn't know why I bothered. I was done with Katrina. She was busy; she had a life, dreams, and work. I had appointments.

"Is it him?" she asked, poking at her own phone.
"Yeah."

—Eleven minutes. No more—

—Say please—

—Per favore, Contessa bella—

ruin.

—Flattery is unnecessary—

—So are your clothes—

"What are you smiling about?" Katrina asked, flopping down the lid of her Styrofoam box.

"Not this burger." I closed mine. "You don't need me for anything, do you?"

"Just stay in touch. Your notes get a little scribbly toward the end."

chapter 9.

THERESA

The Maserati came down Cahuenga and parked in front. Otto's Lincoln must have been dismissed because it was nowhere in sight.

The top was down, and Antonio was in aviators and snug jeans, his boots making a *clup-clup* on the pavement as he came around to open the door for me. "Contessa," he said.

"Capo."

"How was your afternoon out?"

"Thrilling." I sat down, and he closed the door behind me. When he got behind the wheel I asked, "Short notice to give a girl."

"Ten minutes is enough time to get down the stairs."

"Maybe I was busy."

"Were you?" He put the car into drive and twisted to see behind him before pulling out. His leather jacket stretched between his shoulder blades.

"Hardly the point," I huffed.

"Exactly the point." He pulled into the street and headed south with the wind in his hair, the sun on his glasses, and his skin a rich olive color. When he smiled at me, I forgot the point entirely.

"Where are we going?" I asked.

"Back to the east side."

"You won't give up over there, will you?"

"It's mine. I never give up what's mine." He turned to me for a second. "Ever."

"So, if you kept that territory, where did Paulie go?"

He smirked, eyes on the road. I wasn't supposed to ask questions, but if he expected me to stick to that, he was sorely mistaken.

"Is he a businessman without a business?" I used air quotes.

"There is nothing more dangerous than a man who has lost everything fighting something he fears."

"What does he fear?"

Antonio pulled onto the 10 freeway. My hair went nuts, spiraling like cotton candy in the wind. He put his fingers on my thigh, pushing my skirt up. I put my hand on it as he moved it deeper, grasping the flesh.

"Tell me," I said.

"Your legs are closed."

"I'm in a convertible on the 10."

"Open them. *Adesso*. I want to feel if you're wet."

"Antonio, really." A big rig came up on the right. If the trucker had been looking out his side window, he would have had a clear view.

"Pull your skirt down over my hand and spread your legs. One knee touching the door. All the way. Don't argue, or I'm going to pull over and spank you for every trucker on the freeway to see."

I was wet. I had to be. I pulled my skirt over his hand and put my bag on my lap. He grabbed his jacket from the back and put it over the bag.

"Good enough," he said. "Open up."

I spread my legs. The city streaked by in swashes of grey, blots of billboard colors, and flecks of palm-tree green. The only constant was the flawless umbrella of blue sky.

"You didn't answer the question," I said. He changed lanes, blinker and all, and slipped his hand under the crotch of my panties.

"*Dio mio*, you are soaked. What were you thinking about?"

He rubbed my clit gently, one stroke along the length.

"Paulie's business." I opened my legs wider.

"Really?" He leaned back and draped his left wrist over the wheel while drawing sticky circles around my opening with his right middle finger.

"No."

"Tell me."

"I was thinking about your mouth."

"*Bene*. What about it?" A BMW came up close on the right, and I ignored it. If I looked at them, they'd look back. The car was red, and I was throbbing.

"Your lips," I gasped. "Between my legs." He moved so slowly I thought I'd explode from the rush of blood.

"More."

"Kissing me. Sucking. God, Jesus Antonio. How can you drive and do this?" I could barely see past the nest of hair whipping around my face, but I saw his smirk clearly.

"The left hand doesn't know what the right is doing." He grasped my clit between his thumb and forefinger, changing lanes again so he could blow the speed limit that much better.

"God!"

"More," he said.

"And you put your tongue inside me, and rub your teeth on my clit."

"You are dirty, Contessa. And detailed. Do you want to come?" He let the pinch go and rubbed with the pads of his fingers.

"Please."

"Sit still."

I caught sight of him, between the spaghetti of red hair, glancing my way and smiling.

"Yes," I said. "Yes."

"Keep your legs open." He dragged all four fingers over my hard clit once, twice, the bumps and ridges of his fingertips a pulsing rhythm at seventy-five miles an hour.

"Yes."

"Keep still. And no shouting." He ran his fingers over me. Even though it was autumn, I was sweating, muscles clenching, nerves firing. My jaw went slack then tightened when he flicked his nails over me.

Without an outlet in movement or sound, I felt everything. My body connected with wires of pleasure, tightening with the orgasm, twisting, my ass clenching, my pussy pulsating for a cock to fill it, grasping for him in waves. The white noise of the freeway was consumed by my own vortex, and any cares about people seeing me disappeared.

His touch got lighter and lighter, prolonging my orgasm. It went on and on. I closed my eyes and got lost in his fingers, my silence, and stillness.

When I finally stopped coming, Antonio removed his hand from under the jacket and got off the freeway.

He put his fingers in his mouth, and when he stopped at the red light, he brushed his pinkie over my lower lip, painting me with our mingled juices.

"You know what made Paulie crazy enough to break everything he worked for?" Antonio asked.

"It was me, wasn't it?"

"Yes. Partly, it was you."

chapter 10.

THERESA

We made a few more turns, but I more or less knew the neighborhood after the night Marina had tried to shoot me. We were probably five blocks from his burned-out auto shop. He was committed to the neighborhood, for sure. If I owned a business on the east side and someone set fire to it, I'd never want to cross the LA River again.

He didn't say much after revealing that I was not only a target for Paulie because of the feud, but the reason for the hostility in the first place. As if he knew I'd need a minute to absorb the new information, he just drove and waited.

"Where are we going?" I asked.

"I'm driving around until you ask what you want to ask."

"I thought I wasn't supposed to."

He stopped at a light and twisted to face me. "Go ahead."

"Can't you just say what you want without me trying to ask the right question? I'm not the lawyer in the car, here."

"Apparently. And your hair is a mess. Your lips smell like pussy. Did someone just finger the hell out of you?"

"Antonio! You're deflecting."

"I am, Contessa. *Mi dispiace*. This has been obsessing me, and the only time I don't feel obsessed with it is when I'm around you. When I'm around you, I want to pretend it's all gone away." He drove, but with purpose, not as if he was killing time waiting for my question.

"This is going to be a constant battle, isn't it?"

He smiled a devil of a smile. His parents had skimmed from the very top of the gene pool to make that mouth. "If you make things into battles, yes, they are battles." He pulled into a narrow alley and parked in front of a garage.

"Why was he scared of me?"

He opened his door. "Come." He went around the car, keys jingling, and opened the door for me.

"I'm being really patient," I said.

"Yes, you are." He planted a kiss on my lips, and I tasted my sex on his mouth, from the fingers he'd licked. "Women scare him. Especially the wild, unpredictable ones."

"Me? Wild and unpredictable?"

We put our arms around each other, and he led me out of the alley and to the street. The row of buildings was connected, and flush with the street in the old tenement style, with storefronts on the first floor and one story of apartments above.

"To Paulie, you are," he said.

He stopped in the middle of the block. The storefront was empty. A large window had crusty bars in front and cracked glass behind. The door was original to the building, which looked as if it has been built just before the depression and not updated since. On the right of it stood another empty storefront that had been updated in a grotesquely ugly way, with chipped brown stucco and a poorly installed vinyl window. On the left was a store with a purpose I couldn't divine, with hours posted and the sign in the door flipped to "Closed."

"What do you think?" Antonio asked as he unlocked the front gate.

"I think it needs a coat of paint."

The gates creaked, and he slapped them home with a metallic smack. "What color would you like?" He fingered a bouquet of keys.

"Capo, what's happening? You can't turn this into an auto shop. It's in the middle of the block."

He opened the door, turned, and flipped on the lights. He repeated a version of his previous question. "What would you turn it into?"

I didn't answer but stepped past the door, onto a linoleum floor covered in grease and dust. Metal racks lined the right; stacked round tables stood on my left. I glimpsed a dark back room that looked like a place where unpleasant scientific mysteries waited to be solved. "A clean room, first," I said.

"And then?" He jingled his keys. He seemed relaxed and happy, leaning on his right hip slightly, shoulders sloped, face waiting for something joyful, and I knew what our visit was about.

"Capo." I took two steps toward him, with my arms out. "Has anyone ever told you that you're sweet?"

His hands took me by the waist and drew me close. "No."

"You are."

His head tilted slightly, and his cheeks got narrow, as if he sucked them in. His eyes were hard and defensive. I remembered who I was dealing with and how little I knew him, but I refused to be scared.

"I don't want a store."

"The shop is close. I can watch you. And you'll have something that's yours."

I wanted to protest that I had plenty that was mine, and I did. I had a condo. I had money. I had three-thousand-dollar shoes. And if I wanted a store in one of the worst neighborhoods in Los Angeles, I could have one very nicely arranged without his help.

I tamped back all of my resistance because the store was a gift, and a thoughtful one. Most men gave women flowers or jewelry; Antonio gave buildings. I didn't need a dozen roses, and I could buy myself a diamond necklace, but I could see the value of Antonio's gift.

But I didn't want a store. I didn't want to be handed a life.

"Can I think about what to do with it?"

"*Si!* It's zoned for food, not liquor, but any licenses you want…" He held his hands out and said no more. I was sure I could get it zoned as an amusement park if I wanted.

That store was his dozen roses and box of candy. It was completely useless. Pointless, even. In a moment of peace, he'd tried to give me what he thought would make me happy.

"Thank you, Capo. Can I take time to decide what to do with it?"

"Of course."

I reached up to kiss him, twisting my fingers together behind his neck. His tongue hit mine, filling my mouth with aggression and lust. His hands went up my shirt, shoving my bra out of the way with his fingers, thumb teasing my nipple as he pressed his hardness against my hip. Would he take me in that filthy store? Knock me against the metal shelves and drag me into the dark back room? Yes. Yes, he would.

He kicked the door shut. And that slam threw me off for a fraction of a second, so that when the other sounds hit, I thought they were echoes of the door. When Antonio threw me to the floor, I thought it was part of his seduction. I was primed for hard, lustful, thoughtless sex.

But the door kept slamming, and his weight on me was not amorous. His breath came in gasps on my neck, hot and sharp, and he held my wrists down hard enough to bruise.

Glass broke, plaster popped, and what I thought was the crack of a slamming door was no less than the constant *pop pop pop* of gunfire. And my body under his, with the threat of death a sudden stink in the room, was on fire.

chapter 11.

ANTONIO

It stopped. I didn't know if the guy with the gun was reloading or getting out of the car to finish us off. So when I had a second, I let go of Theresa's wrist and pulled her up. It was not graceful or chivalrous. I had no time to apologize, and she didn't have a second to ask what the hell had happened. I pulled her into the back so fast she almost tripped. It would have been fine if she had fallen. I would have preferred to have dragged her.

No windows. It was dark and infested with a cloud of flies louder than mere machine guns.

I heard her say my name, a question in her voice. Next, she'd ask who, how, and why. Only the last question had answers.

Because there was no peace. No truce. Because my name was Antonio Spinelli, and this was my life.

"Antonio." She pulled against me when I got to the back door. I yanked her close.

"No questions now." I growled it harder than I should have, knowing I'd regret it in retrospect.

"Your car."

I turned to her. The light from the front room reflected blue on her eyes. I held my hand still on the door.

The car. A blue Maserati, parked in the back like a cursed beacon.

We stared at each other. She was right; we were trapped.

The windows were boarded. I peeked out, holding her hand. She wasn't shaking. She wasn't even sweating, but her lips were parted, and she looked ready to fuck. I considered taking her, but gunshots wouldn't go unnoticed, and a yellow Ferrari pulled up next to the Mas. It was the man himself.

"Stay behind me." I unlocked the door.

"No, Antonio. Wait." She was flushed, but still sharp. Her eyes flashed, scanning my face. Oh, she wanted to fuck all right, and yet, she seemed more alert, as if her arousal was mental as well as physical.

Paulie, who had been a friend to me, sent a chill up my spine when he got out of the car and stood on the hood.

"Spin!" Paulie shouted. "Come out."

"I should go in front," Theresa whispered.

Paulie held up his hands. "I got nothing. I'm unarmed. I promise; I ain't gonna do nothing."

"He'll never shoot me," she said.

Paulie called out before I could answer. "If I wanted you dead, I woulda come in and done it already."

That son of a whore. He knew it would bother me that he had control. And if I asked for concession for Theresa, if I made sure she walked away, it would be perceived as weakness.

"You stay here," I said.

"He knows I'm here. He could have come in the front. Listen."

"I got a news flash out here, Spin." It was Paulie again. Like the buzz of a fluorescent light that you couldn't fix.

"We have to go out side by side," Theresa urged.

"Listen to me," I said. "Do not speak. Do not make a move. Do not insinuate yourself. Do you understand?"

"Antonio, but—"

"You will stay behind me, not because he'll shoot either one of us. If he kills me, he's a dead man, and he knows it. If he touches you, his life isn't worth anything. But if you come out at my side, I will look weak. Do you understand?"

That last statement was a lie. I wanted to protect her in case Paulie had lost his mind or brokered a deal for my life that I didn't know about. A man has to live with himself and God, and I'd already alienated God.

"Behind this wall right here." I touched the wall by the doorframe. "Stay in arm's reach."

I tried to remind myself that that was Paulie out there. That was a guy who had helped me avenge my sister, who laughed at my pronunciation then helped me get it right. That was a guy who'd thought of us as partners from the minute he met me at the airport. He jumped down from the hood of the car then pulled his gun out of the holster and dropped it in the front seat.

The *thup-thup-thup* of a helicopter came over the distance.

"They're coming, Spin. Come on. We got about five minutes."

I opened the door. It was brighter outside than I'd expected, and I fought to keep my hand from shading the sun. It would look like a sudden movement.

"Come in, then," I said.

"Where is she?" He kept his hands out, an unusually wise move from him. I would have shot him dead if he'd reached for a pocket.

"You try and kill us, and you want to know where she is?"

Theresa stood right at my side but behind the wall, unmoving. I could smell her perfume and shampoo. I could hear her long breaths and the ticking of her watch.

I did not sense fear on her.

If she'd been scared, I might have moved too quickly or made a rash decision. If she'd been whimpering or crying after being shot at, I might have put a bullet in Paulie without a second thought. But she wasn't afraid. Thank God for her.

"I aimed over your head," Paulie said. "I was trying to get your attention."

"You were always impulsive. Always reckless."
He grinned and looked at his shoes for a millisecond.

I'd enjoyed and feared his impulsiveness at the
same time. He'd been valuable, but I'd so often had to
smooth over an overzealous shakedown or unnecessary
insult that, in the end, I stopped letting him manage
politicians by himself.

He still needed me. But I didn't need him, and that
scared him. He wasn't breaking with me because of his
ambition; I had to remember that. This break wasn't
about money, and it wasn't about power. It was about
fear.

"I wanted to tell you something. It's gonna hurt,
Spin. Gotta admit."

"About?"

"This thing we have—"

"You," I said. "This is your grudge."

He admitted nothing. He'd already said everything
he was going to say the night he burned the shop. He
wouldn't tolerate me with a woman so deep in the
establishment's pockets. He would never trust her. He
would never trust me. I had to choose between him and
Theresa. I tried to understand why he'd make such an
ultimatum but came up empty-handed.

"You heard about the Sicilian virgin's fiancé?"

"*Stupido*?" I said.

"Nice Neapolitan kid. But yeah, a little dumb. He
and his girlfriend just washed up in Malibu. You know
why? He refused to marry a nice Sicilian virgin
because he already had a girlfriend. *Stupido* is right.
Made enemies on two continents.

"And?" I didn't want to talk about it in front of Theresa.

"Numbers Niccolò. Our accountant. He's mine. I'm the future of this side of town. You know why?"

"Is that what you shot at me for? The accountant?"

"Niccolò's playing the odds. I got the bloodline for the virgin. She's mine now that *stupido* is dead." Paulie glanced up. The helicopters had gotten closer. "I know you're there, Princess," he called out. He jumped from the hood of the car to the uneven ground of the alley. "Don't get too comfortable. This asshole's shit's gonna be mine in a few months." He got too close. Not to me, but to her.

Something took over me. It was the old Tonio-botz, the man who wasn't much more than muscle, bone, and rage. Even if Antonio was a thoughtful man, Tonio moved quickly because he didn't think.

Paulie had never seen that side of me. He didn't know how swiftly I'd react to him addressing Theresa, even if there was a wall between them. He didn't know I didn't give a shit about his restraint, and he didn't have his guard up when I grabbed the front of his shirt. The defense came up, but it wasn't fast enough.

I heard the *thunk* of his head on the brick wall. When he tried to push away, I leaned all my weight on him.

"Don't talk to her, Paulie. Not a word to her."

It was too late. She came out from behind the wall and leaned in the doorframe with her arms crossed.

chapter 12.

THERESA

Had I gone through my adult life without once thinking I was going to die? Had I never been threatened? Never almost been in a car wreck? Had I never been in the wrong place at the wrong time?

When Antonio threw himself on top of me, while his chest rose and fell as the gunshots broke the windows, I knew I'd never tasted life as closely as I had with that man. The blood rushing between my legs, the juice collecting there, every point of light in my life dropping to that point was painful in its speed and intensity. I thought I'd explode from the desire for his cock before a bullet could even touch me.

Then it stopped, and all I could think about was his mouth and his neck and his sweat, scented with worry and adrenaline. I knew we were in grave danger, and I'd follow him through it. I'd follow him anywhere.

I'd followed him through the store, my ears dulled from the shots, while outside, Paulie waited with his threats and talk of the virgin, the wedding, and a poor, stupid boy sold into a marriage he didn't want and who was killed along with the woman he loved.

Even after that, when Antonio pushed himself against Paulie, close as a lover and angry as a pit bull with the stink of savage rage coming off him, I didn't panic because I didn't need to. All my passion, rage, panic, and arousal stayed tightly confined behind a hard black shell.

Antonio and Paulie were evenly matched, physically, but my Antonio was stronger in his fearsomeness and clarity of purpose. He would never back down, not until he stood over his enemy in victory. His determination was clenched in his jaw and held fast in his fists.

Leaning in the doorframe with my arms crossed, I saw the meaner man take advantage of the weaker one and the force of their bodies against each other, the intensity of Antonio's face, the force of his arms, and I wanted those tight lips and that rigid cock between my legs.

"Antonio," I said.

"Get inside," he growled, his fingers resting on Paulie's cheek and tensing, tensing, until a shadow of a divot appeared in the skin. Their bodies were so close they could have been one person.

"This what you like, Princess?" Paulie grunted. "You like a thug? You think you can make him into a gentleman?"

Antonio pulled his gun out and leaned it against Paulie's head. "I should kill you for what you did already."

As if knowing where his bread was buttered, Paulie relaxed his body and kept his eyes on me. "Theresa, you see what he is? Go back to your lawyer. It's safer."

"Contessa. In*side*."

I didn't move. I couldn't. He was going to shoot him. It was clear as day.

Antonio leaned his elbows on Paulie and chambered a bullet. "This is for the good of everyone," he said.

"After what we been through, it comes to this? You're going to shoot me for a woman? I killed for you, man. I stuck a dead dick down a dead throat for you."

"Antonio. Don't." I was whispering, but I knew he heard me. At least, his ears heard me. There was nothing less than murder in his eyes. "Please."

"I wish I coulda tasted that magic pussy, Princess," Paulie said. "Must be something."

"Inside, Contessa. Don't make me say it again."

I stepped back into the doorway, into the shadows, shaking my head and mouthing the words *don't do it don't do it*...

"Pray, Paulo," Antonio said. "Say it with me. *Ave Maria, piena di grazia.*"

I could still see them in the slit of light between the jambs. Paulie cringed. "The Lord is with thee."

Antonio stepped back and aimed the gun.

"*Tu sei benedetta fra le donne.*"

"And blessed is—" Paulie's voice hitched, and he continued. "The fruit of thy womb, Jesus." He leaned into the wall, but sagged, eyes shut tight.

"*Santa Maria, Madre di Dio, prega per noi peccatori.*"

"Now and... now and..."

I stepped into the sunlight, softly. Antonio had moved backward, to the Ferrari. He leaned in the window and quietly removed the gun, his own weapon still trained on his partner.

"Finish, Paulie."

"At the hour of our death."

Paulie opened his eyes.

"*Amen.*" Antonio pulled the trigger. A spray of brick dust flew out of the wall above Paulie's head, dredging his hair, and he barked a sound that was neither consonant nor vowel but a mingling of both.

Or maybe I made that sound.

"See?" Antonio said. "I shot over your head."

Antonio grabbed me by the arm and pulled me out of building. The last I saw was Paulie stumbling back as if he couldn't believe he was alive.

Antonio practically threw me into the Mas, taking off before the helicopter got over us. I had my hands over my mouth to stifle all the emotion that wanted to spill out.

"Contessa," He rolled the top up and drove slowly and legally. "What?"

"He's right," I choked out. "If something happens to you, it's my fault."

He pulled over, slammed the car into park and took my wrists in his fingers. "Listen to me."

I couldn't see him. I couldn't see anything. It was all too big. Too overwhelming. He was ready to shoot his best friend, right there, for me.

He pushed into me until all I could see was his face, his hands cupping my cheeks in my peripheral vision. I inhaled his smell of burned forests and charred cities, his voice of salted caramel. He was my world, right then, and my heart rate slowed.

"Listen. To. Me." He took a deep breath, and I felt it and mimicked what he did, calming myself by tuning my body to his. "I am responsible for the years of my life," he said. "Nothing you do will change them. This position I'm in is my own. And now, you're in it. We can talk about that later. But now, do you hear the sirens?"

I listened. Nodded.

"The shop is almost a kilometer away. We have only a minute to leave or we're going to be found here."

"We didn't do anything. We were just standing—"

"If I'm here, there are questions. If I'm not, there are layers of paperwork between those shots and the owner of the building."

The *thup-thup-thup* of helicopters was a few blocks away, over the store. Paulie would have left the scene, and we were just two people in a parked car, but we couldn't ignore the impending descent of the law.

I took a long blink. The crisis was over, and there were only three things left: Antonio. Me. And God.

Could I keep two realities in my head at the same time? Could I believe he was good and sound, even though I knew he committed murder while he was with me? I feared it would become too much, some day. The struggle would eat my soul until all that was left of me would be my body, the physical manifestation of ache, need, and desire.

chapter 13.

THERESA

I knew there would be ramifications to Paulie's near-death experience. I'd have to deal with all of it, and yes, I was going to have to deal with my responsibility in his current state of affairs. I breathed once, twice, and I put my fear, arousal, and self-loathing behind a thick shell of ice and control. I knew it swirled underneath, an ever-growing, self-propagating ball of hysteria.

The size and power of that ball terrified me. Once we were in the car, I hardened the shell around it. Blinked. Breathed. Swallowed. Became myself.

Antonio drove like a model citizen. The police sirens died out; the *thup* of the helicopter faded away. I could tell he was trying to be calm and to breathe evenly. Eventually, his grip on the wheel loosened, and he leaned his head back on the seat.

"Will they find us?" I said. "Or Paulie? Or anything?"

"The building is owned by an offshore trust." He took a pack of cigarettes from his jacket pocket and poked one between his lips. "The police will find nothing. The insurance company will get a bill." He offered me the pack, and I declined. He pocketed it and pulled out his silver lighter. "Case closed." He lit his cigarette and snapped the lighter shut with a *clack*.

Antonio drove. Smoked. I wondered if this would be our new small talk. Instead of the weather or the financial markets, would we share a quick description of police activity and the traceability of ownership?

Since the Mas had been parked in the back, no one would know it had anything to do with the shooting. If they did know, they expected it there. The possibility that everyone in the neighborhood kept silent for their own protection occurred to me.

Antonio coiled like a spring, pushing on the steering wheel, even as he drove like the sanest, soberest man alive.

"I am going to fucking kill him." He slammed the heel of his hand on the steering wheel. "What did he think he was doing? Son of a whore. He could have killed you."

"I'm fine."

He put his hand on my cheek. His touch lit my skin in a crackle of firing nerve endings. "I'll rip him apart if anything happens to you. If he scratches you, I'll drive a knife into his heart. Do you hear me? He'll be dead before he hits the ground."

I groaned. I didn't want him to kill anyone, but I didn't want him to stop talking. "You don't need to kill for me."

"Killing him would be kindness if he hurt you." He curled his fingers into a fist. "If anyone hurts you, I will kill them."

Our lust was all mixed in with viciousness. I wanted to take it and swallow it without reservation, even if I blew apart from the intensity of it.

I took his hand and put it on my breast. "What if you hurt me?"

"*Basta.*"

"Take me, Antonio. Hurt me bad." I slid my hand between his legs. He was hard.

He turned a corner, and I saw the yellow-and-black East Side Motors sign. It had a dusting of soot on the bottom. A trailer with a logo for LoZo's Construction had been pulled onto the lot, a man sat in the back of the truck, feet dangling, eating a sandwich. Charred wood and plastic were piled to the left; burned-out cars had been moved to the right. The office side of the building was burned to the beams. The garage fared better, though there had been some damage. Antonio pulled into the garage. It stank of grease and flame. Thickness and sharpness stung the back of my throat. If black had a smell, it would be the inside of that building.

Antonio got out of the car and lowered the gate, shutting the space in darkness except for the wall connecting the office, which had burned off at the top.

I got out of the car, feeling my way along the side of it.

"Antonio? I—"

I felt him beside me a second before his hand grabbed a handful of hair and bent me over the hood of the Maserati, holding me there.

"You want it to hurt?" He pulled my skirt up and dug three fingers into my pussy as if he owned it.

"Yes, yes. Do it." I was pinned. He yanked my panties down halfway then put his wet fingers back inside me without warning.

"If you scream, there's no one in here to hear you. And you're going to scream loud enough to bring the rest of this building down."

I pushed my hips against his fingers, feeling violated and needy at the same time. I needed him to go deeper, to touch me where it hurt most. I was going to break from the inside out of he didn't bend me into nameless shapes.

He took his hand off the back of my neck and pulled my thighs apart. A gust of air cooled the wetness between my legs. He spanked my ass.

"Open your legs."

I didn't have a chance to obey before he kicked my knees apart. His tongue descended on me, the flat of it taking me from clit to asshole. His fingers worked inside, gathering moisture as his tongue worked my clit, not gently, but sucking like he meant to eat it, teeth grazing painfully, leaving waves of pleasure behind.

"Fuck me, Antonio."

"Not yet." He sucked on my clit then licked it, drawing his tongue over my ass. I'd never felt anything like it, and I cried out.

He used his fingers to wet my ass while he gave his tongue to my clit, sucking hard, then licking.

"I'm going to come, you fucking—"

"Come."

"Make it hurt!"

He shoved two fingers into my asshole and I came, pulsing around him, arching back and pushing my pelvis against the car.

"Stay still," he said when I shuddered and twitched. His cock slid into my ass, which was smooth from saliva and pussy.

"Yes!" I shouted. "Fuck!"

"Does it hurt?" he said in my ear then bit my shoulder.

"No." I wanted to hurt, to break, to get lost in pain. I was crusted and black, hardened to steel on the outside, while inside, a molten swirl grew every day I was with Antonio. The pressure of it bloated me, and the gunshots in the store had only tightened my hard-bitten skin into a translucent, paper-thin shell. He had to break it. He had to crack me and let it spill.

He jammed himself in harder, but I was too ready and too needy to think of the stretching as anything but pleasure.

"Do it until I break," I hissed. "Make me cry." I swung back at him, but he took my wrist and twisted it, pinning it against my ass.

"You're going to cry, Contessa. But not in pain."
He put my knee over the hood of the car, and he got in
even deeper, groaning. He went slowly, rotating his
hips gently.

"You won't weep from being hurt. Not from me.
You're going to shed tears from coming so hard you
forget who you are. And when you return, you'll
remember you're mine, and you'll cry then too." He
pumped me hard, once, and I screamed in surprise.
"And you'll cry again."

"Harder."

He didn't go harder; he slid carefully out and back
into my ass, letting me feel every inch of him. I cursed
him. He intended to make good on his promise but
took his time with it, shifting my hips downward until
my pussy was pressed against the hood of the car. It
rubbed against the hard metal.

"You think you want me to hurt you. You don't
even know what that means." I felt rocking, rocking,
his hips and mine, the hood of the car, his hand holding
my arm back, the escalation of pleasure on my clit, my
empty pussy throbbing for something to fill it. "You
have never tasted death," he said into my ear softly, as
if it were a secret.

"Make me taste it." I heard the desperation in my
own voice, the pain of need.

"I can't bring you back."

"Put it on my tongue. Take me all the way. Please."

"No," he said.

In the dim light, his face close to mine, I saw his
jaw clench, his eyes get hard. He pulled me back by

the throat and put his other hand between my legs. I don't know how many fingers he wedged into my cunt while his dick was in my ass, but I was full and covered too, with his warm wrist on my wet clit and his body above mine. I felt protected under his thrusts, even if I'd never be safe again. I let myself crack. The fissure opened and the molten lava poured, pressing against the blackened case of control, smashing it until I screamed as if I were being rent open.

I was made of heat. The cold shell shattered into sharp-edged chips and floated away in the fiery river. I was consumed so completely I screamed in the pain of loss and pleasure of emptiness.

Antonio, the catalyst for my dissolution, the destroyer of my façade, put his lips to the back of my neck. I didn't know who I was anymore, but I was his.

And I wept.

chapter 14.

THERESA

Two bathrooms had survived the fire. Antonio let me take the nicer one. I washed up and came out sore and emotionally drained. I didn't have a thought in my head, only a need to see him.

I heard him before I saw him, rattling off in Italian. I'd never had a talent for languages, but right then, I wanted to learn to speak to him in his. I wanted to sing with him to that same song, to tell secret jokes in the same melody.

I followed his voice to his burned-out office. He was freshly scrubbed and brushed, poking a charred two-by-four with the toe of his dress shoe. I kissed him. His mouth was minty and soft. His face was clean, and when he touched my cheek, his tenderness was a balm on the damage he'd inflicted with those same hands.

He said a few short words over the phone and clicked off.

"What would you say if I sent you away?" he said.

"Sent me away?"

"Back home. My home. I think if I can't protect you, my father can. Until things blow over here. Or until I can go back there."

"There is no way, Capo. No way in hell. I have a family here. I have friends. I can't just get sent away. It doesn't work like that. And I won't be away from you."

"If Paulie ends up running an empire, whatever happens will be my fault," he said.

"The last thirty-four years are my own. And the last couple of months are mine, as well. If something happens to me, it's not your fault. It's mine. I own this."

"No. You don't. I dragged you into hell. Now I have to get you out in one piece."

He put his arm around me, and we looked through the space where the window had been, onto the broken glass and carbon chips that made up his shop, like an old couple on a porch, reminiscing about how the neighborhood used to be.

"What are you going to do?" I asked.

"About?"

"Your accountant?"

"Dime a dozen."

"He went to Paulie?" I asked.

"Everyone loves a winner."

I leaned against a circular-saw table and crossed my arms. Antonio put his hands in his pockets.

"You just nearly blew Paulie's head off," I said.

"Give me credit. If I wanted him dead—"

"And he shot at us."

"He was aiming over our heads." By his tone, I could tell Antonio wasn't defending Paulie but mocking his excuse as one would mock a child who blamed his baseball bat for yet another broken window. "Asshole. I don't want to kill him; I want to rip his heart out."

"I mean it. We have a deal."

"I know, Contessa. We have a deal. I hope to God that you live to be the most beautiful old woman in history."

"I need you to end this, Antonio. Before I lose you. This has to stop."

I put my arms around his waist, and he held me so close I felt the blood in his veins.

chapter 15.

THERESA

I woke up the next morning in a panic. My rib cage felt like a twisted coil around my lungs. I needed to get out of bed, or my spinning brain was going to lift me six inches off the mattress.

I couldn't think about Antonio, where he was or who he was meeting. He'd conducted his business his whole life without getting killed. I had to assume he knew what he was doing.

Daniel was a talking head again. Polls were looking better, but the outcome was touch and go. The local elections were scheduled for March. Four months. I knew Daniel. He wasn't done with Antonio and me. He was gathering clouds for a February storm.

My phone buzzed. I snapped it up without even looking at the caller.

"Tee Dray," said a familiar voice.

"Directrix. How is it going? Do you need me?"

"Uh, yeah. Have you ever been in for questioning?"

"By whom?" I asked.

"LAPD. I lost half a day of edit."

"What did they want?"

"Why don't you come by? I have some questions about your notes. It would really speed things up if I had you around this afternoon."

***

Katrina hadn't been sheltered as a child. Her parents hadn't had a lick of money until middle age, and by then, their daughter had been exposed to enough of the realities of Los Angeles. She knew how to answer questions from the police, something I'd given exactly zero thought to my whole life.

"What happened?" I whispered as she walked me down the hall.

"Remember the day your hot boyfriend came with food for the crew?"

"Yeah?"

"They wanted to know about that." She stopped at the editing-bay door. "They wanted to know what he was wearing, where you went for dinner."

"What did you tell them?"

"Everything." She opened the door.

She went in like it was nothing, and I got in behind her and slammed the door closed. We were alone in the darkened room with only the blue light of the monitors highlighting the curves of her face.

"Like what?" I asked, my tone an accusation.

"What?" She shrugged. "He came. He brought dinner. To seduce you, I figured. And nice job, by the way…"

"Were they asking specifically about *me*?"

"They're lawyers. They don't need to ask. But yeah, that's what they were getting at."

I tapped my fingers on the back of the chair. There was an equation at work, with Daniel sitting to the right of the equal sign.

"He said he was done protecting me," I said. "Looks like he meant it."

"Have you done anything? What happened with Scotty?"

The loan shark Scott Mabat, had shaken down Katrina for her post-production money, threatened her life, refused payment, and eventually run afoul of Antonio. He'd landed in the hospital and was back on the street in a week.

"I pointed a gun at his head and pulled the trigger." I said it as if delivering the news at nine. Who knew what looking death in the face had done to him? If he'd felt threatened enough, he might have gone to the cops, which would have eventually led him to Daniel.

"You what?" Katrina said.

"It wasn't loaded."

"Okay, Tee." She held her hands out as if pushing me away. "This is way, way out of my league right now."

"I didn't shoot him."

"What do you want, a cookie? Holy fuck. Holy fucking fuck. You're pulling triggers on people?"

"He was going to hurt you," I said.

"Oh, no. No no no no. Just, no. I would have gone to the cops."

"And lost the movie?"

"Which I'm going to lose anyway, right now, if my script supervisor and the woman financing postproduction shoots people. Holy fuck, no! They can freeze your assets. Then they can stop post. Everything here can go to hell! God dammit, Theresa!"

"Next time someone threatens to gang-rape you, I'll just give them your address."

She growled, closing her eyes and clenching her fists, as if the anger inside her had to be released before she could say another word. "God, Tee Dray!"

Quick as a snake, but with better intentions, she wrapped her arms around me, squeezing my elbows to my sides.

"Can you lighten up? I can't breathe." I pushed her away. "Did the lawyers ask how you were financing post?"

She pulled back and dropped into a chair. It swiveled and squeaked before stabilizing. "No."

"Then why do you look so guilty?"

"They asked if Antonio was involved with the movie. I said no. He just brought dinner that one time, and it looked as if he was trying to get into your pants. They asked if he did, and I said I wasn't sure. And before you get upset, that's the best answer to give them, because it's all about the doubt, and since I never saw you actually doing it…"

"I get it," I said.

"So, they asked every detail of that night, and if I'd seen him again, and I told them I saw him at your loft the night you banged up your car."

I sat down. I had entered a non-emotional state, and I just took in everything she said. Much could be missed if I got upset or let her push my sympathies.

"From beginning to end, Directrix."

"They said Scott went to the hospital. He wasn't coherent for days, but when he started talking, he implicated *me* in getting the shit beaten out of him but wouldn't say anything else. Now, I was at my parents' place in Orange County, and there's a credit-card trail and a dozen people who saw me getting drunk at my old hangout. So, first they threatened me, but I knew they had nothing. Then they started asking questions about you and Antonio. I denied everything because I never thought you'd be involved. And I still can't believe it. Still."

She looked at me as if I'd just lied when I'd told her what had happened in the shipping container.

"Wait, wait," I asked. "Did they come because they wanted to know about Antonio's involvement? Or because they wanted to know if you had something to do with that scumbag getting beaten up."

"You said scumbag."

"Why did they come?"

She swiveled in her chair and hit the spacebar on one of the keyboards. The monitor flashed brighter. She faced it.

"They were fishing." *Tap tap tap*. I was being shut out.

"Katrina."

"I don't know you anymore. I mean, I thought at first it was all crap. I thought they had it all wrong about everything. You know, like it was just Danny being a dick. But you? *You*? You scare me."

When she looked up at me, her eyes were big and scared and determined all at once. She'd grown up with good parents in a bad neighborhood and had a healthy fear of anything illegal. "This is all I've ever wanted my whole life. I had it and lost it. I'm getting it back. My job. My work. This movie is happening. I can't let anything get in the way."

"Is my financing it getting in the way?" It hurt to even say it. Giving her money felt like the only productive thing I'd done in my life.

"I don't know," she said.

"Fine. We'll talk about this later."

"Don't be mad."

"I'm not. I understand. I can't…" I swallowed. I could barely continue. "It's not right if I sully your work."

"It's not that." She turned toward me then away.

"It is, and you know it," I said.

"I keep thinking it would be easier if I could just get a studio to back me again. Even without LAPD hanging over the thing and the paper trail back to a loan shark. Michael's amazing. I might cut together a trailer and see if I can get Overland behind this picture. The odds are impossible, but what the hell, right? I mean, after I got Scott involved like some film-school amateur, I deserve the problems I've gotten. It's my responsibility to get out of them."

"Just let me know." My voice must have been thick, because she stood up and put her hands on my shoulders.

"I don't want to hurt you."

I backed up. I didn't want her hands on my shoulders, and I didn't want to talk anymore. I felt filthy, and I had a compulsion to leave before she saw the depth of my wickedness.

She was worried about hurting me, but she had it backwards. I was the one who wound up hurting her every time I tried to help her. God damn Daniel for not just leaving her alone, and God damn me for not finding a way to shut him down. I went downstairs with my head held high and my shoulders lowered from the weight on them. Otto opened the car door for me. I was a princess with unearned graces, a sparkly package with a bomb inside. I couldn't live like that. I couldn't go about my business and watch people get hurt without taking action.

When Otto stopped at a light, I leaned forward. "Are you going to eat lunch?" I asked.

"Now that you mention it…" He patted his stomach.

"How about In-n-Out? You can get me an Animal Style."

His eyes lit up. "Great idea."

I know I smiled, but I was so angry I could barely think. I transmitted none of that in my face or body language. I knew anyone who saw me wouldn't know what was going on in my mind, or sense my heart palpitations. Except Antonio. From day one, he knew what my body was doing when no one else did. Good thing he wasn't there to see me thinking through what I wanted to do to Daniel.

Otto pulled into the lot, and while he was waiting on line, I slipped away. I didn't like doing it, and I knew he'd get into trouble, but I needed to breathe and to make my own decision about how to handle Katrina.

chapter 16.

ANTONIO

I tried to make peace with Paulie because Theresa had asked me to and because she was right. Doing things for Theresa's sake was getting to be a habit.

Donna Maria Carloni agreed to broker the peace, and surprisingly, Paulie agreed to show up. I'd been Donna Maria's *consigliere* for two years, and I was convinced Paulie wouldn't let her broker anything. I was wrong.

I never should have been in the life. My father saw that it would eat me alive, but from the minute I walked in to him and demanded vengeance for Valentina, and he took the demand from me and gave it to one of his men, I was in. I didn't even want to be, but I had changed, and the power and freedom that came with being *camorristi* became a need. He had no other way to protect me from myself and from the people coming after me.

Since then, not one second of my life had been my own. I was the property of Benito Racossi, his *consigliere.* His right hand, protected and enslaved. Then I moved on to be Donna Maria's *consigliere* as payment for a debt. I was never my own man.

I must have been confusing for Theresa. I had to appreciate that. I was reluctant to expose her to the life but, at the same time, drew her in. I worshipped her virtue while destroying it. I murdered men even as I feared God's justice. My mother had told me that a man who held the idea that he was good in his right hand and the knowledge that he was damned in his left was destined to live half a life.

The hills were a sunbaked brown and dark grey-green, thick with brush and spotted with chunky rocks, like Naples, without the ever-present shadow of *Vesuvio,* still and silent but boiling inside.

I turned in to a nondescript dirt driveway that any casual observer would have missed, which led to the ass end of Whittier Narrows. No one was supposed to live there. It was a preserve, not meant for residences, but Donna Maria Carloni's dead husband had worked it out forty years ago and created an inviolate right-of-way. To attack Donna Maria, a person would have to trespass on government land, and then pass a gantlet of cameras. She ended four underbosses with her own hands to regain her husband's perch at the top of East Los Angeles's mafia pyramid.

I made a hand sign to tree-perched camera: one thumb pressed against the center of my pointer finger, where the scar was. The white gate appeared a hundred feet later with another camera mounted on top of it. It opened.

A quarter mile along the brushy dirt drive, I tipped my head right, then left. The still unripe fruits of the olive trees hung heavy. The last time I'd been there, two weeks before, they'd been harvesting on rickety wooden ladders. I'd been politely summoned and told that Vito had to be dealt with. I found him trading in pictures of girls—babies—and threw him hard enough to dislocate his shoulder. We didn't do that. *Camorristi* did not keep prostitutes or traffic women. We did not make money on the backs of children, and we did not ever sexualize them.

But although that was offense enough to get Vito killed, what broke my crew was the valet parking. Men opened little businesses like that to make extra cash. It was a simple thing, but ended with him betraying Paulie and me.

He started the valet business to do something honest. The little shit pedophile was trying to go legitimate, and for that, for doing what I wanted to start but didn't think I could finish, I destroyed him. I let my temper get the best of me. I chased him. I shot at him. I pulled him out of his house in Griffith Park and threw him down a hill. And from that point on, my reputation as a man who kept control of himself and his crew spiraled downward. It happened faster than I thought it could.

In the weakness came an opening, and in the opening, men's ambitions flowed. One man's ambitions made him chase Theresa down the freeway to kidnap her. Another trapped her into attempting murder.

A *camorrista* accepted that death could come at any time, for any reason. The sins of a boss were visited on his crew. It was a trade we accepted. We could be killed, but our families and our women wouldn't be touched. And when I became the boss of our corner of Los Angeles, I grew eyes in the back of my head to watch for the knives.

The *camorristi* didn't answer to Donna Maria, but we didn't ignore her either. We did our business because if we actually had the desire to band together, it would be more trouble for her to fight us than to take the loss.

The house lay low to the ground with a corrugated tin panel jutting over the doorway. Potted succulents and cactuses covered the cracked concrete and walls. From the outside, with its rows of citrus trees on the right and left and the sweet smell of the olive trees, it felt like being back in Naples.

I got out of the car. The alarm went on with a chirp. Useless automation. There was no safer car in California.

"*Consigliere*," came a voice from behind me. I didn't turn around but put my hands out, palms in front.

"Ruggero," I said. "That's not my job anymore."

I felt his hands on me, checking my shoulders, waist, back, and heels. He was a big guy and a pussycat. Even though I faced the other direction, I know Skinny Carlo was next to him. Skinny Carlo was sixty-five kilos, drenched in seawater, but he was responsible for much of Donna Carloni's dirty work.

"You run around unarmed like one." Skinny Carlo had a voice like a serrated knife.

"I left it in the glove compartment." I turned and flipped him the keys. They twirled in the sun a second before he snatched them out of the air. "It's loaded and cleaned. Treat her nice."

"We wasn't expecting you for an hour. She's not seeing no one," Ruggero said.

"Right."

I walked into the house.

Donna Maria was not interested in how things looked. She preferred misdirection. So, her home looked like a Sicilian ghetto house, decorated with faded floral curtains and browned crocheted table coverings underneath chipped porcelain figurines of children. She'd had eleven babies and had shipped them all back to the mother country to be educated.

I walked through the dark house to the backyard. I was convinced she slept in the dirt somewhere on her eight acres.

The sun seemed brighter back there. Not just vivid, but merciless. Stacks of hutches on both sides stretched back into a distant orchard, and in the wood and wire boxes were animals. There were rabbits to the right and, to the left, small creatures with fur so sleek they could only be minks.

In front of me stood a table three feet high with wood sides and wire mesh stretched over the top. The mesh was crusted with black.

The boss of the biggest Sicilian family east of the Los Angeles river was a handful of sticks wrapped around the middle with twine, no taller than five-two and starvation thin with hair that had more salt than pepper. She made her way to us with the surefootedness of a woman whose feet hadn't bothered with pavement in a while. In her right hand she carried a twitching white rabbit by its hind legs and, in her left, a two-foot shaft of hard wood. As soon as I saw it, I took my jacket off and draped it over the back of a chair.

"*Consigliere*," she called out. Even though we both spoke Italian, I could barely understand her; the Sicilian accent was as thick as tomato paste. "I expected you."

"I'm here, but you have no *consigliere*."

"There are no Italian lawyers to be had. Not for love or money." She wiggled the rabbit back and forth. It squirmed a little, dropping its ears.

"American ones know the system well enough." I rolled up my sleeves. This was not particularly messy work, but I still needed be cautious, and I couldn't avoid the work altogether. If I demurred, I'd lose the advantage of my lineage and culture.

"I won't lower my standards." She handed me the club. It was blacker on the business end and slicked brown and smooth on the grip side. "Americans are weak and mouthy. They don't show respect, and they die with secrets on the way out of their mouths."

She held the rabbit out over the wire-mesh table.

"They love life too much, Donna." I tapped the back of the rabbit's head, getting my aim right, favoring accuracy over strength. It was the only humane method, and if I hesitated for one breath, she'd notice. This, like everything, was a test.

"And you," she said. "Do you like running your crew more than sitting by my side?"

"I do." I brought the club to the back of the rabbit's head, where the ears met the neck. The death was soundless, with only a hollow thud to alert the universe that it had happened.

"You were doing fine at it, too." She held out the rabbit and let it bleed out of its nose and mouth onto the black gravel. "Until a couple of weeks ago." She shook it a little, letting the last of the blood fall away.

"I had it under control." I took the dead rabbit from her and held it over the grass by its heels as she twisted a valve on the side of the house and picked up a hose. "I admit I failed with Paulie. I didn't expect him to turn on me."

"That's very grown-up of you. And that's why you made a good *consigliere*. You know when you fuck up." She hosed down the rabbit until its fur was matted and flat, and there was no blood on the surface. I turned it so she could get the back, letting the fouled water drip onto the gravel until it flowed clean. She shut off the hose, and I put the rabbit on the grate.

Back home, small animals peeked out of the ruined mountains to peck at the garbage and city families were so poor that a piece of meat didn't get away just because it ran fast. Despite my father's position, my mother had run the house as a single parent, and rabbit and raccoon were frequently on the menu.

"So," she said, opening a small knife. "You came early for the rabbit cacciatore, yeah?"

"I came here for an indulgence."

"Ask." She passed me the knife by the handle side. She wanted me to do the honors. That was her way of saying I was favored because of my background, and to refuse would be to throw her favor back in her face.

"I have a woman." I cut the skin inside the rabbit's thigh and up to the gut.

"I've heard." She smiled and took out a beedie, a short, black cigar with a smell that reminded me of the garbage piled on the side of a Neapolitan highway.

"She's a good woman."

"She was in bed with that *sbirro*."

I slashed inside the rabbit's other thigh, right through the animal's penis. "That's over. She's loyal to me." I held the rabbit's hind legs and yanked the skin off it then looked at my boss with the inside-out animal in my hands. "Once this thing with Paulie is done, I don't want her looked at or questioned. She's with me."

"You say this is a small thing."

"It is," I protested.

"In America, yes. You can have your personal life. You marry for love. But that's not where you're from. Not with the job you have. You don't own your life."

I cleanly slashed the rabbit's center muscles from gut to neck. Green-grey organs spilled out onto the mesh. I realized I was wound tight from fingers to core. I switched the knife hand and flexed my fingers.

She was a skinny thing, the donna, but she was formidable, ruthless, and protected. Too many men had made the mistake of underestimating her. Even though I knew my fingers could break her neck, those fingers would be attached to a dead man before they even touched her.

"You, *consigliere*, are part of something bigger than yourself." She picked up the hose. "You are a man of traditions. And you are not just any man in this tradition. You are a prince. Do you think a prince can just marry anyone he wants? He has his king to consider. His country. The blood of his children. His own future." She sprayed the rabbit carcass down, and the grey entrails fell onto the mesh. "You want some sweet pussy, you keep it. But you don't marry it. Everyone knows this. You don't contaminate your family or your business."

"Let me worry about my business. You worry about yours."

"I am." She took the carcass from me. "You've heard about my granddaughter and Patalano?"

"Suspected."

"Well, I wanted to be the one to tell you anyway. Paulie Patalano is taking Irene. He's going to be a powerful man. You ready for that?"

"I can handle it." My phone buzzed in my pocket. It was Otto.

"Good. Come inside," she said.

"*Un momento.*"

She went and left me. I picked up. "Otto."

"I'm sorry, boss. I lost her."

I closed my eyes. Jesus Christ. Where could she be going? Why would she sneak away? I cursed everything: my vulnerability, my love, my powerlessness. The only thing that kept me from leaving to sniff her out was the knowledge that Paulie wouldn't do anything while we were supposed to be negotiating a truce.

"Find her. Just find her."

chapter 17.

THERESA

The Downtown Gate Club was in the middle of the
city, down a turn to the left on Venice Boulevard and a
right on Ludwig Street, where the streets took on a
little curve, and the trees shading the rare brick row
houses stood farther from the curb. A couple of blocks
of oddball houses in the last sweet corner of downtown
made the perfect enclave for those daring enough to
make that neighborhood their home.

A person from the north might pass it by without
noticing it. But old-money Angelinos who found Bel-
Air tacky, those born into a level of privilege it might
take decades to wean from, knew better. They knew to
turn down the driveway of a brick building with
stonecarved window treatments that sat ten feet from
its neighbor. The building had been one of a row of
businesses as early as the eighteen-fifties, complete
with basements and stone foundations.

"Miss Drazen," the guard said as he pulled out his clipboard. "You here for the LA Democratic Summit?"

I was, and I wasn't, but I needed to get past the gate, and if he looked at the clipboard and found I wasn't there, he'd let me in but not check me into the Heritage Room. "I'm here for Daniel Brower."

"I just saw him." He opened the gate.

The DGC was visible on satellite, but from the street, it was surrounded by enough houses and foliage that passersby wouldn't notice an eighteen-hole golf course. Transplants didn't know it existed. LA natives knew it was there, but few had been inside. The club didn't try to go stealth; it simply wasn't glamorous or flashy. It wasn't a desirable place to be, outside of certain circles, and the board did everything in its power to stay under the radar.

I left my little blue BMW with the valet. He eyed the dent on the passenger side and said something polite before coasting away. A tall man in a uniform opened the glass and brass door for me.

The Heritage Room was as old as the club, somewhere in the order of one hundred and fifty years old. The walls and floor were stone, and the ceiling crisscrossed with beams the thickness of a ship's mast. The "Heritage" in question was the heritage of success, which tended to follow all its members. Glass cases held trophies, medals, photos, certificates, and plaques from elite tournaments. When my father had brought me there at the tender age of eight, I'd been impressed by the shiny artifacts, the high ceiling, and the marble. I'd stared at the pictures of my father and grandfather, trying to discern the real men through the oil paint and how their own moods and words came through the canvas. But not much came through. The men were painted to erase their Irish heritage. They looked like mouse-haired WASPs. I hadn't thought about the dulling of the fire in their hair since I was an adolescent, and seeing it again irritated me anew.

"Theresa!" Gerry came out in a light-grey suit and dress shoes, smiling at the dozen straitlaced politicians dotting the room. Gerry was Daniel's political strategist. I'd spilled my guts to him one night, when he picked me up from set, and I'd been wondering about the state of my sanity.

"Hi, Ger."

He kissed my cheek and gently led me to the doors that opened out to the golf course, where we couldn't be heard. "To what do we owe this surprise visit?"

"Wanted to talk to Dan."

"He's in the conference room." I stepped toward it, and Gerry put his hand on my shoulder to stop me. "Wait."

"Yes?"

"Let me get him."

"It's fine. I know about Clarice. It's not going to be a scene."

He twisted his face into a half smile that meant he was going to say something difficult. "I know you'd never make a scene. Neither would he. And Clarice isn't here yet. But it's not that."

cd reiss

I crossed my arms. "Describe it, then." A fake
laugh echoed through the room. I recognized the ex-
mayor Rubin right away.

Gerry took a deep breath, calculated to let me
know the conversation was hard for him. "Who you're
seeing is going to get out. Eventually."

"Oh, you're kidding—"

"You can't pretend it won't have a negative effect
on his candidacy. And I'd hate to say this thing is in
the bag so soon, but if—no, *when*—he wins, it's going
to be a pressure point, even if you don't keep showing
up."

"Theresa?" Daniel had found me. He put his hand
on my shoulder.

"Hi, Dan."

He kissed me on the cheek, and Gerry cleared his
throat, looking around to check if anyone had seen.

"Take it easy, Gerry," Daniel said, his hand still on
my bicep.

Gerry smiled and folded his hands in front of him.
"This is lovely. So happy we're all getting along.
Now"—he opened a wooden door with a window set
into it and dropped his voice—"get the fuck out of
sight."

He pushed Daniel past the door but did it gently, by
the hip, so it didn't look like he was being pushed.
Then he closed the door.

The office belonged to the Heritage president, and
some of the oldest medals in the club's possession
were shelved there.

I wanted to break all of them. As soon as the door clicked, I turned on Daniel, keeping my voice at a low growl. "Do not ever, ever send your team of pit bulls after my friends. If you want to know something, you come to *me*."

"This is about the director?"

"Don't play games," I said.

He sat down on the leather couch as if I'd said nothing at all. He'd learned something from me, apparently. I was the one who got calm during a fight, and he was the one who flew off the handle. Well, that was about to change, because I suddenly understood what it meant to deal with a passive aggressive.

"You went to Katrina about Antonio. That is not acceptable."

"You should sit down." He sat back with his arms in front of him. But I knew all about his strategies and body language: the position of his arms and what it transmitted, how he could speak without speaking, and how he could say two things at once. Adopting a pose was a big part of what Daniel and I did together, and hands in front was meant to project a simple honesty, even when it was a lie. "My office is following leads on a money-laundering scam through a restaurant in San Pedro. It's public knowledge."

I remained standing. "I don't want you harassing my friends."

"I don't want you fucking a known criminal while I'm running for office, but we don't always get what we want."

I didn't know what I'd expected. The visit was impulsive. I hadn't prepared Daniel, and I hadn't prepared myself.

"You're turning your professional bailiwick into a personal vendetta."

"Give me a break. You want a personal vendetta? I've got your sister Margie on wiretapping. Your brother has a few shady real-estate deals in his portfolio. Another sister's got two potentially illegal adoptions. And the other one, fuck. What the fuck happened at Westonwood sixteen years ago? And as for your father, don't even get me started on his disgusting personal tastes, which everyone knows and no one talks about. I've had a personal vendetta to protect you and your family, and let me tell you, it's wearing thin. I could take your entire family down faster than I could take Antonio Spinelli down. But I don't because of what we had. Because I respect it. So don't come in here and tell me how to do my job."

I threw my bag down next to him and stepped forward until my knees were in front of his. "Daniel, let's talk about respect. What it means."

I leaned over, putting one hand on the arm of the couch and one on the back, bending until my lips were at his ear.

"Tink, please." He tried to push me away, but the effort was halfhearted.

"Respect isn't treating me like I'm made of sugar. Because I'm not. I'm made of cum and saliva. I'm made of salty sweat, and I taste like fucking. I sound like an orgasm that's so hard you can't even scream, and I fuck like a closed fist."

He turned to me until his breath was on my cheek. I heard him swallow.

"Do you want me?" I knew the answer. "I can feel your fingers twitching. You want to stick them in me. You want to see if I'm wet. You're confused because I don't usually make you this hard Because you *respect* me. Women you respect don't make your balls ache."

"Jesus, Tink." He was barely breathing.

"You're hard."

He reached for my breast, and I caught him at the wrist and pinned it to the back of the couch.

"If you knew me, you'd respect me. If you respected me, you wouldn't threaten my family. And you wouldn't even breathe my lover's name."

He deflated, though his dick was still rigid under his trousers. I stood straight.

"Since we're doing threats, let's talk about the illegal campaign contributions, the filthy texts. There's enough borderline stuff I know about you to sink your career. But if you fuck with me, it's going to be my civic duty to tell the *LA Times* about how I helped you with your struggles with overseas taxation."

"You wouldn't."

"Fuck with me," I said. "Please. I want you to. I want to shed a tear, telling the *Times* about how we opened accounts for the express purpose of your tax efficiency two weeks before you lobbied to pass laws against them."

I crossed my arms and set my mouth. We stared at each other.

"This sounds like an impasse," he said.

"Then we understand each other."

I backed up and reached for the knob. Quicker than I would have thought possible with that rod of an erection, he got up and put his hand over mine. "How is he going to react to you being here? Is he going to be able to hold himself together long enough for you to win his war for him?"

"You're implying I'm being used?" I asked.

"Implying?"

"Dan, you don't know the half of it. And it's not my responsibility to tell you anything." I pushed my bag farther up my shoulder and faced the door, putting my fingers on the seam at the jamb. "But I will tell you this: he is genuine. Maybe not in the ways you care about, but I've never been loved the way he loves me. He loves me recklessly, to the misuse of everything else in his life. What kind of woman would I be if I let him get careless for me?"

"He's playing you."

"He's not. I've been used before, and it didn't feel anything like this." I stole a glance up at him. I'd hit him just where I wanted to.

A soft knock came through the wood of the door. I looked through the frosted glass to the light-grey shadow of Gerry.

"We're on," Gerry said.

Daniel opened the door.

ruin.

I said a few hellos to the people I'd known in my past life as they filed into the conference room, and I walked out unscathed.

chapter 18.

ANTONIO

I could smell the rabbit cacciatore from the yard, where I swirled a jelly glass of sweet wine and walked along the rows of hutches. A slinky mink nibbled on the wire of her cage, and I leaned down to stroke her nose. Paulie was due in fifteen minutes. We'd make a cautious peace. He'd marry Donna Maria's granddaughter and run an empire. And then?

Then, I'd make the impossible happen. I'd get out. It had to be done. Even if I got out of Los Angeles to avoid Paulie, I'd be expected to continue in the life, and Theresa would never fit. The only option was to secretly unwind everything in my life and live the rest of it out with her. I didn't know when or exactly how. I didn't know if it would be done during peace or war.

But I knew it would be done. Then my Contessa could be released from the cage I had to put her in.

Far in the front of the property, I heard a car engine get louder then stop. It was Paulie, undoubtedly. I didn't react to knowing he was there, close enough to shoot at me again.

Fabric rustled behind me, and I turned. "Hello," I said to the girl before me. Her mane of dark curls contrasted with her white shirt. She had Donna Maria's brown eyes, without the hardness.

"Hi. Grandma said I should come and see if you wanted anything."

"Anything?"

She shrugged and smiled. "Sure."

I handed her the empty jelly glass and spoke to her in Italian. "You're from Sicily?"

"*Si.*" She took the glass. "I mean, no. I was born here, but I've lived there since I was six."

"And you're how old now?"

"Twenty."

She looked about that, with her lips parted in a smile and skin so smooth she looked like a painting. She looked as if she'd never cried a day in her life. She reminded me of Valentina, my wife, and I was blindsided by the memory. She had been one of the truly beautiful things in my life, before I became everything my mother tried to stop me from being.

"What's your name?" I asked.

"Irene."

"I'm Antonio."

"I know. Grandma said."

"What else did she say?"

She smiled and looked away then looked up and swung her hand out, speaking English in a thick Italian accent. "'Go find the man outside and get him something. Stand up straight. He is Antonio Spinelli, a prince. Treat him like one.' Then she threw me out."

"I'm no prince."

"*Camorrista* from a long line? Kind of prince-like."

"A bastard son."

"Or just a bastard?" She kicked a hip out and shot me half a smile.

"For such an innocent-looking girl," I said, "You flirt shamelessly."

"At home, I don't get to. My mother won't let me look a man in the eye. Here, it's expected. I kind of like it." She looked me in the eye and waggled her brows. She was cute. We walked back to the house slowly, hands in pockets.

"What you're doing is very dangerous," I said. "If you pick up bad habits here, the boys back home will start talking. Then they'll start doing. It's not flirting anymore after that."

"You sound like my father." She flashed a pout worthy of a 1940s Hollywood drama.

"He's a wise man."

"All business." She waved me away. "Cigarettes and gasoline. But he won't let me smoke or drive."

I laughed. Poor kid. Then I realized she'd told me her father's businesses, and thus, her lineage.

"You're Calogero Carloni's daughter?"

"Yep. The Princess of Sciacca! I want to die. Jesus."

"Hey, watch your mouth."

She puckered it in response.

"Why did you come here?" I asked. "To Los Angeles. College?"

She laughed. "You don't know?" I stopped and she stopped with me. We faced each other. "There's a wedding in a few weeks. I'm expected. So are you, I'd think."

"I never miss a wedding if I can help it."

"I got a light-blue dress," she said. "What color are you wearing?"

"Haven't given it much thought."

She shrugged and turned on her heel. I noticed her feet were bare. "Someone else was here for you. Should I bring the wine to the dining room?"

"Please."

She went ahead of me, her hips flirting with me while her face was turned away.

I walked back to the house. As if a box had opened and giggles came out, it was suddenly populated with children. Three ran past, screaming and bumping, none taller than waist high. They joked in pidgin Italian from deep in the south of the boot and colored with Anglicisms. I swore I heard one say, "Dude," before rattling off a series of baseball stats.

"Don't shoot."

I heard Paulie's voice but didn't need to look around. "You'd be dead if I wanted you dead."

"Yeah, yeah. I don't expect an apology."

"I don't owe you one."

Donna Maria shuffled in from the dining room. "You two quit it."

She slid open a big wooden pocket door, revealing a small study with heavy chairs and dark fabrics. A deeply masculine room, it looked inherited directly from her late husband.

Paulie went in first. Two men were at either side of the window. They had risen to their feet when the door had opened. One was Skinny Carlo; the other was a clean-cut gentleman in a full suit, about forty years old. I didn't recognize him.

"Carlo," I said as Paulie sat.

"Spin," said Carlo.

I turned to the man I didn't know. "Antonio."

He didn't say anything. The cuckoo clock over his head ticked loudly. I could hear the gears grinding.

Donna Maria shuffled in. "Don't mind him."

"I'll forget to mind him when I know who he is."

"He's from the old country."

"Mine or yours?"

She laughed to herself. A clear, crystal Virgin lighter, about the size of an eggplant, wobbled when she sat behind her desk. It had a brass metal head that flipped up to reveal the flint. These things made better paperweights than lighters, but that didn't stop old Italian ladies from buying them. I'd seen about a hundred of the monstrosities in my life.

"There's only one, but if you have to know..." She waved her hand at the stranger.

"Aldo," said the man. "From Portici. I'm sent to make sure this runs smooth. So we don't have any trouble with our friends from the south." He spoke in an Italian I knew well, the spiraling tones of my hometown clicking together like gears.

"I don't need to be watched."

"He ain't watching you." Donna Maria sat back in her chair, her body filling in the worn spots in the leather. "He's watching me. Ain't you, Aldo?"

Aldo didn't answer.

"All right. Let's get down to it," she said. "This thing with you two, it's bad for business. Not just your business, but mine, because if I gotta get into it with you to keep the peace—"

"It wouldn't be a peace," Paulie interjected.

"You can put it back in your pants. As an interested third party, I'm just here to make sure all's fair and send you two on your way. I don't need to tell you that what's done in here is done. What's agreed is law. What is said is true under God and the Holy Virgin. Yes?"

I made the sign of the cross. Paulie and the two men sitting behind Donna Maria did the same, even though it wasn't their job to agree; it was their job to listen.

"*Bene*," Donna Maria said, fingering a piece of paper. "We got a nice chunk of territory east of the river and north of Arroyo Seco. Biggest hunk of camorra territory in the country. You guys got tobacco, real estate, protection, and something happening with a garment factory on Marmion. Good job, that. No tributes to pay, either. Nice to be Neapolitan."

Paulie snickered. I lit a cigarette with my own lighter. She didn't know all of what we had, but she didn't have to. She only had to know that within our territory, she could push all the drugs she needed without interference, and though she didn't officially run prostitution, she managed to squeeze cash out of a few pimps working in the soot of the 110. We split the local councils and brokered the bigger politicians individually. When shit broke out with the gangs, we negotiated the area as a solid block. It was a good system, and I was invested in keeping it intact. We loved peace. Peace was profitable.

"I have a proposal," I said. "Geographic. Split at the railroad tracks. I take east."

"You take west," said Paulie.

"The shop is mine. What's left of it."

"Split along the foothills through Avenue 37," offered Donna Maria.

"That cuts the commercial district by half a mile," Paulie said. "Do this. He gets three blocks at the edge of the foothills, and I get the outer ring up to the river and the arroyo"

"Fine," I said. That gave me the garment factory and the shop. That was all I needed in the end. He could have the commercial sector if he thought he could make any money off it.

"When he bails on us, I get his stake," Paulie said.

"What?" I said.

"*Eh?*" Donna Maria said.

Oh, that son of a whore going to try and corner me. I should have shot him when I had the chance.

"See how easy this was?" Paulie continues, holding his hands out to indicate the room, the people, the agreement. "I would say, normally, he's just going to grease me first chance he gets, but he woulda done that yesterday if he coulda." He turned to me. "I ain't afraid of you. I'm a made man. If you take me out, you're gonna lose your dick. So I been trying to figure what you're doing. Sat up all night, thinking. Tick tock, all night, listening to that clock, and it wasn't till the sun came up that I realized. You're getting your shit in order. You want out of the life."

There was a dead silence that was filled with the ticking of the cuckoo clock and the laughter of the children outside.

Donna Maria laid her gaze on me. I didn't have to answer the charge, serious as it was. I didn't have to entertain the challenge or defend myself. I could leave it hanging with a laugh and a wave of my hand. But with Donna Maria looking at me, and the clock ticking over Aldo's head, I knew I had to counter the charge.

"Let me tell you something. My great-great-grandfather carried a *carabina* for Liborio Romano when the *Atto Sovrano* was nailed to a tree. And not a generation has passed without an olive tree being planted for us. Not one grows that my grandfather didn't oversee the pricing, and my father, even now, fixes the price of every kilo. My family is in the orchards, from the roots to the leaves, and you think I can run away from that? The blood beating in me is

Napoli. It's this life. I'm *camorrista*, blood and bone. And do not ever, ever bring anything like that up again. It's an offense to my father and my father's father."

A heavy silence followed. Even the children were quiet. Only the clock went on and on.

Paulie leaned on the arm of his chair and stroked his chin with his finger. I know I betrayed nothing, but he was a little too confident. "I know who you are. And there's another piece of this deal. You drop the *inamorata*."

Donna Maria broke in. "We don't discuss the women, Paulo."

"That's the deal, or I'm out. Theresa Drazen goes."

"You can't lead like this," Donna Maria said. "You'll end up dead."

"Well." Paulie fingered his phone. "So you know, it's not just 'cause I don't like her face. It's because she met the district attorney at the Downtown Gate Club today for a private chat."

I burned from the inside, as if my spine were a fuse, and my heart was a bomb; the spark coursed from my lower back upward.

"You're lying," I said.

"I ain't. Got this text right here from a good source. Gerry Friedman from the mayor's campaign." He held up the phone for Donna Maria. She put reading glasses on and read while Paulie continued. "He wants her to fuck off, too. She's poison. But that's besides the point."

I didn't want to see his fucking phone. I didn't think I could read a word of it through the haze of rage I was holding back. I didn't know what she was doing with Daniel, but I wouldn't have her tried and found guilty by that *stronzo*.

"My split's east of Cypress Avenue," I said. "And south of Merced."

"What?" Paulie twisted in his seat to face me. "You can't redraw this now."

I looked at Donna Maria when I said, "Yes, I can." She did not flinch. This was going her way, I realized.

"No, fuck you." He shot up, pointing at me, looking at Donna Maria. "What's this asshole playing at?

Normally, the person who stands first has seized the power in a negotiation. My father taught me that, but I taught myself how to change that without getting up.

"Ask him," Donna Maria said.

"What the f—?"

He didn't have a chance to drop the curse before I swept his legs from under him. He lost his balance and caught himself on the edge of the desk. I swiped the crystal Virgin from the desk and hit him on the temple. Blood sprayed on Carlos's shirt, but he didn't move, even when Paulie went flying into the sideboard. Dishes fell, Paulie grunted, yet I didn't hear a peep from behind me. Just our breathing and the ticking of the cuckoo clock.

"It's all mine, you *stronzetto*. All of it."

I pulled him up by the collar. His eyes rolled to the back of his head, but he reached and slapped me. I barely felt it. Theresa had slapped me harder.

"Come on, Paulie. This is too easy."

I dropped him, and he caught himself on the sideboard, wobbly. I almost felt bad. He'd been a brother to me until he broke with jealousy over a woman.

"You're a dead man," he grunted, his hand reaching for the bloodied lighter that I'd put down. I moved it an inch farther away. He reached again.

I looked back at Donna Maria. She had her arms crossed and was leaning back in her chair as if the TV was playing a rerun. Carlos was smiling, and Aldo frowned but hadn't moved an inch. The clock ticked as always. I turned back to Paulie, who seemed to be getting his bearings.

Paulie's fingers touched the blood-streaked crystal Virgin. Her head had fallen off, and she was just a lower half with a butane lighter sticking out of her.

I moved it another inch farther. "How many times will I have to make you pray before you understand?"

He didn't answer but hitched himself up. I put my weight on him, pinning him under me. Stuff rattled on the shelves. I picked up the statue and put it in his hand.

"You mention Theresa again, I'm not going to kill you," I said, wrapping my arms around his neck and pressing his artery shut. "You're going to beg to die."

He became dead weight in my arms, and the crystal Virgin fell out of his hand. I picked it up.

"I've cleaned blood off that thing twice already," Donna Maria said.

"Third time's the charm." I poked a cigarette out of the pack and lit it with the Virgin Mary's brass butane head. "He'll come around in a few minutes."

"I'll deal with him," Aldo said.

"You got other problems," Carlo said to me. "This woman. The one he's talking about?"

"Yes?" I suddenly didn't want him or anyone to utter her name.

"You going to do something about it?"

"Yes, but I'm going to have to miss the cacciatore. My apologies to your daughter."

chapter 19.

THERESA

I wasn't in the habit of going to church anymore. It was a requirement before I turned eighteen, but once I got to college, I could beg off with studies and activities a little too easily. Once I was in my twenties, no one pretended the requirement would stick.

I still knew what to do. Stand up. Sit down. Kneel. Stand. Kneel. The standing and kneeling seemed strategically placed at the end of the mass, when legs got wobbly and the evening's fast made attention hard to keep.

Margie stood next to me in a *contrapposto* pose, as if she were simply too impatient to be in that big stone box with its waxy smell and bleeding Jesus.

"You called me here to tell me you're worried?" I whispered. "Why didn't you just call me?"

"I needed to see you. And now I'm worried more."

Margie always had a sense of when things were wrong with us. Back before I knew how to get in trouble, it amused me. She could take one look at Fiona and know when she was using, or talk to Jonathan for ten minutes to know he was having trouble with his wife. The only one she couldn't read was Daddy. But no one could read him.

"I'm fine."

"I heard you went to see Daniel today."

"Jesus—"

"*Shh.*" Her hush wasn't drawn or loud, and sounded more like *chh* than a soothing naptime sound. "Will is watching you."

"Watching me?" The church broke into song, and we stood, the organ drowning out our words, and the voices of the crowd keeping me from hearing the pounding of my heart.

"He's good," she said.

"I don't want to be watched. I'm a grown woman."

"Too bad. We need to talk, you and I. Right after communion."

"No."

The woman in front of me turned around to glare, and I glared right back.

"You are in deep, playing the DA against the mob, you're—"

"Shut up, Margie. Just shut it. I'm not talking about it with you, ever."

"I will not sit back and watch you destroy yourself," Margie said.

Every muscle coiled, every breath came short. I wanted to yell, to push, to fight her on everything. I wanted to say words that would cut her, about her spinsterhood, about her lost opportunities, about her authority to mother any of us.

Luckily for Margie, the woman in front made it her business to shoot us a librarian stare, and I got to funnel my anger into her.

"Turn around and mind your business," I said.

Margie looked at me as if I'd lost my mind, and maybe I had.

I didn't smell burned pine when he stepped next to me, probably because of the weight of the incense. Nor did I feel his closeness, probably because the nave was packed, but when he put his hand on my arm, and I felt the lightning of his touch, I knew it was him.

"Contessa," he whispered.

I looked up at him. Gorgeous thing in his jacket and shirt, hands gripping the pew in front, all squared-off knuckles and throbbing veins. Those hands needed to be on my thighs, clawing my back. Even in church, I had ungodly thoughts.

The hymn ended, and everyone sat in a rustle and clatter.

"She's worshiping, for Chrissakes," Margie said.

"Good," Antonio said, snapping up a bulletin. "So am I."

He knew the words, as did I, and we recited the responsives until Margie seemed distracted.

"I have to talk to you," he said.

"OK." I pushed against him, feeling him next to me, his solidness against my tipping form, rocking with the music as if the rising phrases of the hymn made him denser and made me more viscous.

"Were you at the DA's office today?"

I went cold. My skin curled in on itself, and the backs of my thighs tingled with an adrenaline rush. The music sounded as if it were being sung through a funnel.

"Not the office. I saw him at a club."

We faced each other, standing in church with our hymnals open. "Was this an accident?"

"It wasn't what you think."

"What do I think?" he asked.

"You think I want him, I—"

He took my hand and pulled me out of the pew. Margie looked more irritated than frightened, and I shot her a smile to keep up the ruse but then yanked back for half a second long enough to say to my sister, "Never. And stop asking."

But I admitted to myself, as he pulled me out to the vestibule and down the marble stairs, I was afraid. I didn't think he'd hurt my body, at least not in a way I wasn't begging for. He could, however, hurt me with his anger, his disappointment. And though I hadn't given the trip to see Daniel a second of thought, I probably should have.

"Listen!" I yanked back at his hand at the bottom of the stairs, but he yanked me and swung me through a doorway.

ruin.

The choir dressing room was ancient with wooden lockers built in the Depression. So, when he slammed me against them, there wasn't a clatter of sheet metal, but a *thunk* as my body rattled.

Antonio grabbed me by the wrists, locking them together in two fingers and holding them over my head.

"You think I'm worried about him?" He put his finger to my face. "I spend not one minute of my life thinking about that man with you. He's not even a man. He's not worthy of you. He's one of a thousand rats on the bottom of a sinking ship."

"Then what's the problem?" My question came out in a gasp because my body gravitated toward him, arching to press against him, just as he arched in the opposite curve to keep his face close to mine.

"Why did you see him?" I could have kissed him, but I moved my head against the locker door, turning my face toward the arched lead-glass window. I wanted him, not in spite of his anger but because of it.

"He went to Katrina. His team grilled her, and I don't like it."

"What did they grill her about?"

He knew damn well, but he wasn't going to assume. I noticed that about him. He never assumed anything or jumped to a conclusion.

"You," I whispered.

"Me."

"You."

"And you told him what?" he said.

"To stop. To leave you alone. That if he didn't, I had enough on him to make his life a living hell."

"Do you think you maybe should talk to me first, before you do crazy shit?"

"No." I twisted and pulled my hands down. He let them go but increased his weight on me, pushing me against the lockers. "You barely let me out of an apartment that's not even mine. I highly doubt you'd let me see Daniel."

"Because it's stupid and dangerous."

"It's what I have to give. And it's useful to you. And go to hell if you don't like it. I will never, ever sit still while he's after you."

"I'm already going to hell. *Grazie*."

I pushed him away, and he grabbed my jaw, holding me still while he put his nose next to mine and spoke into my mouth. "You're a loaded gun. Do you see that? You're from a different world, but you smell like home to me. I haven't been to Napoli in ten years, but whenever you're near me, I smell olive flowers. My heart gets sick with thirst, but the water is poison."

"Antonio—"

"I'm drowning, Contessa."

"What are you talking about?"

His face got tight, holding back a flood of emotion. His fingers pressed harder on my face until I took hold of his wrist, pulling it down. He let go.

"Talk to me," I said. "Just tell me."

He looked confused for a second. Overwhelmed. Then, as if the dam had burst, he wrapped his arms around me and put his mouth to mine. It happened so quickly that I didn't kiss him back at first. I couldn't breathe; he held me so tight, but I got my arms around him and my mouth open, pulling him close, pushing as much of myself as I could into whatever part of him was within my reach. Thighs, hips, hands, shoulders, lips bashing lips, tongues forceful on tongues. It wasn't even a kiss, or at least, not like one I'd ever had before. It was a slap, a punch, the use of force, a coercion of two worlds into uncomfortable cohesion.

The kiss never got soft and only ended when he jerked himself away.

"Talk to me," I said in a breath.

"The thing I want most is the only thing between me and getting it. You are everything that will destroy me. I should go back to who I was. But you made me dream I could be free, when I'd forgotten I was in prison."

"Is this about you being honest? Is it about me seeing Daniel? Antonio. If I hurt you, just tell me how. Let me make it right. Let me help you get out."

He caressed my face with both palms with a tenderness that shouldn't have been able to contain such intensity.

"Sweet olive blossoms," he said. "That was God's message to me." He stepped away, and the space between us became a sigh. He held his hand. "The only way out is through."

chapter 20.

ANTONIO

I wanted to kill her. I wanted to worship her. I wanted to fuck her. I wanted to fill her so deeply she broke from the pain, screaming my name.

There would be no end to the trouble. She would cause it then escalate it then make it impossible for me to change my life enough to make it stop. She was dangerous, undefendable, and powerful in her own right.

She was going to be the death of me, and I was suicidal. I would kill for her, or I'd be killed by her, but no matter what, someone was getting anointed in oil and put in a pine box. God willing, it would be me and not her.

I kept the top up and the windows closed after the church. I was still at a rolling boil, and she sat back and said nothing, about that or anything, as I drove her up the hill to my little Spanish house. It was in slightly better shape than when she'd seen it last. The walls were plastered, but there was dust everywhere. The kitchen had been ripped out and the bathrooms were down to the bare necessities, but the bedroom was beautiful in spite of all the mess.

I'd tried to integrate her into my life before, but with half measures. I'd introduced her, thinking it would shield her, and it did, as long as my crew was my crew. Once that broke, she wasn't above getting hurt for betraying us, nor was she considered one of us. I was back to square one, and only when she admitted to seeing the future mayor did I realize how vulnerable she was.

I'd protected my wife. I'd protected her life, her virtue, and her ignorance. In the end, only her virtue survived, and I knew in that church basement that it was the most useless of her qualities. Only her life had been worth saving, and I'd failed at that.

Had Valentina known about my history, my father, and the world I'd turned my back on, she might have been more careful. She might have known what to look for. But I'd treated her as if she were an amusement park: a separate world, free from reality, where I could pretend I was something I wasn't.

I didn't want that for Theresa. I couldn't leave her. I was not a good man. I wasn't even decent. But with her, I could find an honest place in the world. Because she was worldly and sophisticated but still virtuous, I knew she could teach me to be the same.

In the seconds when I held my Theresa's jaw and she kept a firm grasp on my wrist and looked at me without fear, I recommitted to my plan to become a better man. I would have her and leave the life my father had denied me and that I'd rushed into despite him.

She was the only one who could take me there but only if her eyes were open and only if she wanted us as much as I did.

I didn't even want to think about it, but I had to. Tomorrow. Now, I was drunk on her scent, smelling the orchards of my youth, when I was just a fatherless child and not the end of a long line of bastards.

chapter 21.

THERESA

We snaked up a familiar hill. He'd been quiet the whole drive, only acknowledging me by taking my hand and squeezing it. At a red light, he looked at our hands together. I wanted to ask him what had changed, but the light went green, and the car took off.

The only way out is through.

I didn't know what he'd meant, but in saying that, he'd changed. He got tender. He kissed my lips and said, "Come home with me?"

I didn't know where that was, but it could have been old Napoli for all I cared. I would have gone anywhere.

"I'm sorry, Antonio. I wasn't trying to cause you trouble. I was trying to help you and Katrina both."

He didn't answer explicitly. He could have said it was all right. He could have shrugged or kissed me again. In the end, I let him take me to his car.

"Why here?" I asked when we stopped at the end of the drive at the Spanish house on the hill.

"This is my house." He opened my door and led me out of the car and up to the house.

"I thought the place on the east side was where you lived."

"Before this house, I had the small place for me." He unlocked the door and swung it open. "I got this because I realized I wasn't in this country temporarily. I was never going back, so I thought I'd settle in. Act like I really lived here."

"I like it."

"Good." He put his hand between my legs, wedging it. He bunched my skirt in his fist and curled a finger over my crotch. "Because I'm about to fuck you in it. You ready to scream?"

"I think we should talk," I said, not really meaning it. I wanted him to take me before he could tell me something I didn't want to hear. My legs opened to take his hand, and my skin tingled.

"After. We have plenty to discuss after."

"Capo," I whispered.

"*Sei mia.*" He got his finger around my clothes until he found where I was wet. "*Questa è mia.*"

"What does that mean?" I asked. My hair was still a nest of wind, and it stuck to my lips when I spoke.

"This"—he slipped his fingers over my pussy—"is mine." He put his other thumb in my mouth before I could answer, pressing my tongue down, and once he moved it I said. "*La tua bocca è mia.*"

I nodded and pressed my lips around it. He tasted like church when he slid his finger from between my lips. When it was out, I said, "My mouth?"

"Mine."

I couldn't take it anymore. I unfastened his pants and we kissed. I was at his command, no matter what he wanted, no matter what his plan.

He pushed me to my knees, and I collapsed to a kneeling position, looking up at him when he put his thumb back in my mouth. I stroked his cock, so thick and ready, the thumb a small piece of flesh in comparison. "*La bocca,*" I said.

"*La mia bocca,*" he replied. "My mouth. *È tua.* Is yours."

"*La mia bocca è tua.*"

"Excellent. Now I'm going to use what's mine."

I opened my lips, and he took them.

He was cruel. He put his cock in my mouth and held my head still while he pushed forward, down my throat. He shoved past my gagging, past my breath, and I let him. When he let me go and drew back, I sucked in air, paused, and then looked up at him.

"*La mia bocca è tua.*"

I opened my lips to let him take me, let him fuck my throat raw. He took a handful of hair and pulled me forward, sliding his cock in my mouth, stroking the bottom of it on my tongue.

"*Sei mia,*" he growled between his teeth then pumped down my throat again. The bottom half of my face dripped with spit and throat gunk, but still, he kept his cock in my face. It was uncomfortable, painful, degrading, and yet my nipples hardened and my panties were soaked with wanting more.

When he was as big as I'd ever felt him, and his firmness matched the weight of my ache, he took his cock out of my mouth and held it there, the tip almost touching my lips.

"*Apri*," he said, eyes at half-mast. "Open."

I opened my mouth, and he started to come into it, leaving a bitter trail on my tongue. He pulled out and moved against my face, coming on my nose, my forehead, groaning into it, until he looked down at me and smiled.

"Oh, *Dio*, Contessa."

"You like it?"

He chuckled and kneeled with me. I smiled, and semen dripped in my mouth. I laughed. I couldn't help it.

"You look like a wedding cake." He wiped his thumbs across my cheeks.

"It doesn't really come off." I licked my lips and wrinkled my nose. "And it doesn't taste like cake."

He laughed, rubbing the moisture down my forehead and across. "I anoint you in the name of the father, the son, and the holy moley."

I laughed so hard I nearly choked, and he laughed too, even as he tried to wipe my face with his undershirt. I put my face up against his chest and wiped it all over him and laughed so hard tears rolled down my cheeks.

"Woman!" He pretended to be angry but wasn't. Who could be angry while laughing and wearing a shirt covered in spunk?

He picked me up and threw me over his shoulder, singing some Italian song on the way to the bathroom, while I pretended I didn't love it.

He put me on a pink-tile vanity built in the 1950s and ran hot water over a washcloth.

"What happened before church?" I asked. He opened my legs and settled between them. "You didn't just barge in because you had a bad dream."

He wiped my face tenderly with the hot cloth. "I had a meeting with Paulie and the head of the Sicilian family that runs the east side."

"What was it about?"

"Splitting territory. That's how it started." He kissed my damp cheeks, one and then the other, then gathered my shirt at the hem and pulled it up. "Arms up."

I put my arms up, and he peeled the shirt off.

"Did it go okay?" I asked.

"It went fine. I'm not worried about territory. I only have to make it look like I'm worried." He unhooked my bra, and I wiggled out of it. "I have to be at full attention. I have to rebuild the shop, take care of my men, and make good decisions."

"I sense there's a 'but.'"

"But I'm preparing to leave. I'm thinking about it every day. Then Paulie announces you're sitting with your ex, in a room."

"It wasn't—"

He put his finger to my lips. "Basta, woman. I know you're not going back to him. I own you, remember?"

I nodded.

"No one trusts you. They think you're going to sell me out, and then they'll be next. So, we hear you're with him—"

"Gerry," I said. "He made the call. He's got contacts with the city council in your neighborhood. I have a feeling you know the politicians pretty well, too."

He smiled. There was a world of knowledge in the way his face fell into it. "Yes, of course."

"Well, Gerry doesn't trust me for the same reasons Paulie doesn't. He made sure you heard all about it." I put my hands on his chest. "I know I didn't grow up with what you did. But you have to know I can keep my mouth shut. I will never betray you."

"You betrayed me already by being there. By not telling me." He put his hands under my knees and squeezed them against the sides of his waist. "I know it was done with a pure heart. But don't do anything like that again."

I bristled at being told what not to do, and he must have sensed my discomfort because he drew his face close and kissed me with those satin lips, flicking his tongue across mine.

"You realize that you just told me stuff," I said. "Real stuff about your business."

"I can't do this without you. I can't even protect you unless I put you by my side. It's the only way."

I didn't know how to answer that because I didn't know what it meant in a practical way, but from his face and his voice, I knew what it meant to him, as a man, as a leader, and as my lover.

"*Come vuoi tu,*" I whispered.

chapter 22.

THERESA

We spent the night in the heavenly expanse of his bed and woke up with the songbirds. The first thing I felt was pain between my legs. How many times had he taken me? Just thinking of it, I felt a familiar ache, and I reached for him, but he wasn't in the bed.

"*Buon giorno*," he said from the side of the room. He was already dressed in slacks and jacket and was pulling his cuffs from under his sleeves.

"How can you be up?"

"I have a lot to do."

"Such as?" I said.

He sat on the side of the bed. "My shop is a wreck. Zo needs to rebuild it. I need to make sure my territory is secure. And I need to prepare a way for us to leave." He slid the sheet off me, exposing my nudity to the morning sun.

"Where will we go?"

"Where do you want to go?" He smirked, running his hands along the length of my thigh.

"With you," I groaned.

"Men die trying to leave because they make it public. So this is our secret, even from your sisters and your friends. Do you understand? It's a matter of life or death."

"Yes," I said.

"You're with me. You're in the life. You are mine for everyone to see. One day, we'll be gone."

"I have a family, Antonio. I can't disappear."

"I know. For now, you're beside me. No one will hurt you."

"You keep saying that."

"I mean it," he said.

"Good. I want to go to Zia Giovanna's. I want to look at the books."

"No." He cut the air with the flat of his hand. "*Assolutamente, no.*"

I sat up straight, naked from the waist up and not caring a damn. "You say you want me to be integrated. You say you know you can't keep me locked up. You say you want to share with me."

"Not in the business. If you do something you can be accused of, your consequence is on me."

"I know Daniel's been looking at Zia Giovanna's. He told me it's part of a fraud investigation. And I know you lost your accountant to that motherfucker in the Ferrari." His eyes widened in shock. I was a little surprised at my language, as well.

"The books are clean," he said.

I got down on my knees, letting the sheet fall from me. "You have no idea what Daniel's people look for. You have no idea what they miss, and you don't know what they catch. I know it inside and out. It's wasteful to not use me." I got up and stomped to the bathroom, turning before I got to the door. "I can fuck a felon, but I cannot fuck a fool."

Lightning fast, with criminal agility, he picked me up and threw me on the bed. I landed on my back with my legs spread. I opened them farther.

"So, felon or fool, Capo?"

He kneeled over me, hands between my legs like he owned everything there. Two fingers in. Out. In. His lips covered gritted teeth.

"You're going with Otto," he said, taking his slick fingers up to my clit.

"Yes, Capo," I groaned as he drew his fingers across it. "But I miss my car. Can he follow me?"

"Agreed. But about the books, you look; you don't touch."

"Fuck me."

"You'll wait." He pinched it and I cried out. "That's punishment for calling me *tonto*."

"Oh, you bastard." My smile belied my words.

He laughed to himself. "At least that. At least."

chapter 23.

THERESA

I felt energized for the first time with him. Embraced. Accepted. Maybe it would even work. Maybe the solution really was to go deeper in. Dante and Virgil needed to go to the deepest circles of hell in order to find the way out.

I bounced out of bed and got ready. Otto waited outside, smoking with his four-fingered hand.

"Miss Theresa," he said.

"Hi, Otto. Can you take me to my car?"

"I'm taking you," he said. "And no running for food. We go; the car moves, and it stops when we get there."

"I'm sorry. I hope I didn't get you into too much trouble."

He opened the back of the Lincoln. "Enough trouble for one man in one day."

I got in. He didn't talk much on the way to the west side but just asked where we were going. I breathed as the city went by. I breathed deep into my chest, inhaling relief and a sense of belonging, if not with Antonio's world, then with *him*.

I opened the door to the loft I shared with Katrina. The air smelled stale and the surfaces had a fine layer of dust. It hadn't been that long since we'd been there, but the lack of activity had a psychological effect on the space. It felt forlorn and empty. I went right upstairs and showered and changed. Forty minutes later, I was back in Otto's car; then I got into the car I'd renamed the Little Blue Beemer and headed east to Zia Giovanna's. The Lincoln followed. I had at least the impression of freedom.

I touched my St. Christopher medal, pinching it between my thumb and second finger. Antonio could guarantee my safety from many things, but he couldn't protect me from derision and dislike. I'd have to turn that around myself.

The restaurant was packed with a lunch crowd, hipsters and businessmen who must have been from the media center down the street and a few moms with strollers parked alongside their tables. I went right to the kitchen. Zia Giovanna scuttled between the row of hanging tickets and the stove while waitresses filed in and out with heavy dishes.

She looked up, saw me, and went back to scanning her orders. "*La Cannella*. He said you'd be back."

"You know why I'm here, then?"

back when the blast of heat hit my face. The wood was good and hot, smoking and red. The paper would disappear in the flames, along with my spotless character.

As I stood by the flames with the documents over it, I paused. Was I really doing this? Was I really going to cross over? My impending action was not just illegal. It constituted aiding and abetting criminal activity. This was jail time. It was my soul in flames.

I hoisted the papers and books to oven level and was about to throw them in when I felt pressure on my arm. It was Antonio.

"What are you doing?" he said.

"Cleaning up the books."

He took the pile of papers from me and closed the oven. He looked stern and almost confused.

"You are with me, but you're not to endanger yourself. We're going to put these back. You're going to watch it. If anyone asks, as far as you know, the boxes have everything. *Si*?"

"*Si*, Capo."

Zia Giovanna pushed him out of the way and pulled the stack of papers from me, muttering something in Italian. When Antonio spoke softly and patted her on the back, I knew he'd accepted an apology.

"Listen to me." He pinched my chin. "That you would do this with your own hands, it says a lot. But those books are clean."

"No, they're not." I held up my finger. "You might know your business, but I know mine. You have income streams at the beginning of every quarter that make no sense at all. Your expenses would break the bank of a corporation. All we have to do is get rid of—"

"*Basta.*" He put his hands up.

"No, I'm not going to *basta*. You're going to *basta*. Either this accountant you had sucks at this, or he was setting you up. I'm going to hope for the former, and you can worry about the latter, but—"

He silenced me with a kiss, a mouth-filling, brain-wiping kiss. By the time he pulled away, I'd lost my train of thought.

"I'm crazy," I whispered to him.

"Sit with me," he said.

"Don't try and shut me up. I want to say what needs saying."

"*Come vuoi tu.*"

A corner table had been set with red wine and bread. Antonio pulled the chair out for me and sat across. "I got us *osso buco*. Zia Giovanna wanted to give you the same sandwich you left on the desk."

"She's tough."

"In her old age, she's softened. When I was small, she held my nose to open my mouth more than one time. And she was a devil with a wooden spoon. I have scars."

"I haven't noticed any."

"You have to look harder next time." He poured wine. "We can talk here. About the books. I'm not an accountant; I can't see what you saw."

"It was bad."

"I want you to tell me, but this is the last I'll hear of it. I don't want you involved."

"You sent me here," I said.

"Not for this."

I took a deep breath. He was stubborn and for good reason. He was right; I had no business in his world. He needed me to stay out, not only to protect my own purity but because my ignorance of the rules meant I could blunder with my words or deeds. And the stakes were very high: prison, or death.

I extended my hand over the table, and he took it, sliding his over mine.

"I don't want to be in your business," I said. "I think it's stupid and dangerous, to be honest. Maybe because I've never worried about money. I've never wanted for anything, so I've never had to consider stealing it or killing for it. But the things I've wanted, really wanted, haven't come to me, either. I'm thirty-four years old, and I've never been married. I don't know how many kids I can squeeze in before it's too late. And everything has a habit of falling down around me. But I don't want this to fall apart. You and I. It's the most impossible thing I've ever been a part of, and if we're not both on board, if we're not both making every effort to be together, it's going to get taken away from us. I promise you, Daniel isn't done. He can take you away from me, and the only thing that's going to keep him off you until the election is knowing that I'm willing to lower the hammer on him. And I will, Antonio. I will. I can end his career. As God is my witness, if he comes after you, I can destroy him, and I will."

"If he fell off the earth tomorrow, ten more would take his place," Antonio said.

"He says the same about you, I'm sure."

The waitress brought two plates of saucy, sloppy stew, and though I didn't want to pause the conversation, I was starving.

Antonio put his napkin on his lap and waited for the waitress to leave before speaking. "This isn't the tradition. Even if you grew up next door, you'd be limited. You have to accept that."

"You said you wanted to be with me the right way. To get out of this whole thing."

"That's between us."

"Exactly. And if we're trying to do the same thing, then I need to help you. If that means keeping you out of jail, so be it. I'd be serving a greater good by getting involved."

He didn't answer but pushed his food around. I couldn't believe what I was arguing for, and there was a good chance he couldn't, either. I was asking him to let me into a criminal life. I was begging to get in so I could get him out. I'd lost my mind, but it was what I wanted.

"Don't think this is easy for me," I said. "I'm of two minds about it. I can't believe I'm asking to commit crimes so you can stop."

He smiled at his plate, pensive. "You keep two opposite ideas in your mind at the same time. It's the only way to survive."

"Let me survive with you."

He put his fork up against the edge of my plate and pushed the plate toward me a eighth of an inch. "Eat."

I put a piece of meat in my mouth. "It's good."

He ripped a piece of bread from the roll and dunked it in the sauce. "Have you ever been to an Italian wedding?" He blew on the hot sauce.

"Are they like in the movies?" I asked.

He leaned over. Holding the dunked bread with one hand and cupping his other hand under it to catch any errant sauce, he held the bread up to my mouth. "Did you know, when Italians came here and opened restaurants, they started serving butter to go with the bread. Butter is a luxury where I'm from, see? So, they were giving what they saw as a luxury."

I bit down on the bread, and he pulled it away while I chewed.

"The expensive places here," he continued, "they give you good olive oil. Which is wasteful. Where I'm from, the bread is for the sauce."

"This has what to do with an Italian wedding?"

"There's the way back home, and there's the immigrant way, which has fake luxury. Tons of it. It's embarrassing."

"Yes, Antonio."

"Yes, what?" he said.

"The Bortolusi wedding." I took another forkful of meat and sent it home with a mouthful of rich burgundy. "I'll go with you."

"I can't take you."

My fork clinked loudly when I put it down. "Are you serious? You think Paulie's going to try something at a wedding? I thought you guys worked it out."

"Doesn't matter. I'm just letting you know where I'll be that day," he said.

I wanted to throw my fork at him.

Having given me the information and laid down the law, he settled into a few bites of *osso buco*. Then he looked at me over the rim of his wine glass and caught my expression. "What?"

"How is this 'getting out by going through'?"

He raised an eyebrow as if I'd just asked him to bend me over the buffet. "Forget it."

"You decide to bring me closer, then you keep me in a box all over again."

"I'm figuring out how to do this, same as you."

"You have to take some risks."

"Not with your safety," he said.

"If you bring me, it will show that whatever I said to Daniel that day didn't hurt you."

"Or that I'm a fool."

"It's business. Your family is undoubtedly in the middle of a negotiation with the Sicilians, but am I right in thinking nothing's locked down yet? As far as the details go, I mean."

"You're right," he said.

"If you bring me, it empowers you. It's going to disarm them. They're going to wonder what the hell you're thinking." I took a bite of meat and chewed slowly. "Also, it'll scare the hell out of Paulie. There's no use in having a bazooka unless the enemy knows you have it. If you want to keep the peace, that is."

He sipped his wine, avoiding my gaze. It wasn't like him. I could have asked what was bothering him, but I had the feeling I knew the answer.

I was right again.

chapter 24.

THERESA

We passed the night in the cocoon of the bed. When I was with him, my isolation was acceptable, simply a way to be close, to hear his stories uninterrupted. He talked about the color of Naples, the veiled identities of the camorra, the family he called his own and the one he inherited when his father came back into his life.

"Your father really loves you," I said, propped up on my elbows. He leaned on the headboard, stroking my shoulder with a fingertip. "He gave mixed messages, I admit. But he only wanted what was best for you."

"He was trying to keep me safe as *consigliere*," he whispered, brushing his thumb over my cheek. "*Consiglieri* are lawyers who advise bosses, so they aren't meant for vendettas. But I had to send a message to the men who killed my wife."

"Did you send the message?"

His lower lip covered his upper for a second. He slid down into the sheets and wove his legs into mine. "You're going to ruin me, Contessa."

"*Rovinato*," I replied.

He laughed. His eyes lit up, and his cares fell off him. I wondered if I'd ever get to see him smile once a day, or even once a week. As beautiful as he was on any given day, he was a treat for the eyes and heart when he laughed.

chapter 25.

ANTONIO

"There's talk," Zia Giovanna said, twisting a fistful of dough into a long beige tube. She insisted on making her own bread at five a.m., even when it would have been more economical to leave the bread making to bakers. "My sister tells me they're whispering over there."

Zia Giovanna's sister was my mother. Both held advanced degrees in gossip and hearsay, so in their garden of chatter, a seed of truth often sprouted leaves and flowers of beautiful lies.

"How can they hear each other over the traffic?" I didn't want to hear her little rumors. I had a ledger spread on the stainless counter. The office had become claustrophobic in seconds. I had rows and columns of numbers to organize since Numbers Niccolò had taken off and left me with them. I wasn't a numbers guy. I could do the basics, but past that, I'd always had people to organize the larger concepts into smaller processes. Niccolò seemed to have done his job of hiding and cleaning money through the restaurant by means of misdirection and sleight of coin. Theresa had been dead right, though. Once she showed me where the trail led, it was very obvious he'd done a terrible job.

"When you came here, I told you to stay away from Donna Maria. Sicilians. You can't trust them. They're animals. You didn't listen. You never listen."

I could do numbers and listen to her scold me at the same time. One took up the attention of my brain, the other, my heart.

"But you run." She pounded her dough, pulling and twisting. "And you sit by her as *consigliere,* and that puts you in her sight. She knew Paulie was going to fuck up. He's American. He can't do anything the right way, the patient way. Even though he wanted Theresa out, he couldn't do it right. A smart man would have waited to marry into the family then taken you out but—"

"*Aspetta*. What are you talking about?"

She looked like she was going to cry. She slapped a ball of dough down. "Paulie's wedding is off. He's weak. They're all talking about you beating him, and they're looking at you to unify the families."

"What?" I said.

"Your father stepped in. He thinks he has you. He says it will be done. His Neapolitan interests and the American Sicilian. You and Irene."

I held my hand up. "Slow down."

"Make this go away." She pounded her dough, flattening the tube in one place. "Tell them you want the red-haired one. She's all right. She won't hurt you. She won't force you."

I couldn't make it go away. I had no way to undo what was done, and if all Napoli was already whispering, it was unlikely my father could undo it without brutal consequences, not just to me, with my disposable life, but to Theresa, who was under my care.

I needed to get out more than ever, and as difficult as that would have been anyway, it had just become nearly impossible.

Was I committed to this? Or was I going to make half efforts? Leaving the life, breaking so many ties, and slipping away was always a nice fantasy when I couldn't find my way through a problem or when the light at the end of the tunnel turned out to be an oncoming train.

After I'd lost Valentina, I'd made choices. I'd gone in with my eyes open, and having made those choices, I never questioned the fact that I'd earned all my own troubles.

chapter 26.

THERESA

Katrina's text woke me from a dead sleep. I swung my arm for Antonio, but he was gone. He'd left me alone in his little Spanish house. He must have trusted me with the silver.

—Can you come to the editing bay?—

—Why?—

It wasn't like me to question Katrina, but I was half asleep, and I missed Antonio already. I should have been thankful that I was out of *The Afidnes*, but I wasn't. I felt like I'd stepped out the door to find the stoop had disappeared and the sidewalk was open beneath me.

*—Because you were a part-time
script supervisor, and you're half
the team that put the half shots in
order and I'm confused right
now—*

—Fine. Give me 20—

Otto waited outside.

"Do you ever see your wife?" I handed him a thermos of coffee.

"It's the arrangement," he replied. "She knows what I have to do, and she accepts."

"She's very generous."

"She is."

"I want to take my car. Can you follow to the post-production place?" I helped up two fingers. "No burgers, I promise."

He agreed to follow close, and I let him, not making a move to lose him. I knew his proximity relaxed Antonio, and that was important to me.

"What's up?" I asked Katrina when she opened the glass door.

"Nothing." She wouldn't look at me.

"Nothing? Describe 'nothing.'"

She walked a pace ahead, looking at the floor. "The type of nothing that's just unpleasant." She reached the door to her editing bay and put her hand on the knob.

"Katrina?"

"I didn't have much in the way of choices," she said. "I had wonky location permits and my financing was, you know, questionable."

"You don't need to review a shot list. That's what I'm getting."

"I hate my fucking life. Really." She opened the door.

Daniel sat in the biggest chair, one leg crossed over the other at the ankle.

This was how a poor kid from Van Nuys got to be a mayoral candidate. First, he showed up where he wasn't wanted, and he was ready. He was armed with information, and he had a plan. He surrounded himself with people who could help him, and he cut the rest of them loose. He was ruthless in his pursuit, hungry, careful, and above all, shrewd.

"Sorry, Tee," Katrina said.

"It's fine. I have this."

This was how a poor kid from Carthay Circle became an award-winning director. First, she did what other people wanted, as long as they stayed out of her way. She understood the hierarchies of power as they related to her singular goal. She understood personalities and could make judgment calls about how to play them for and against each other. She apologized for it, and she never pushed far enough to make enemies, but she knew how precarious her situation was, and she protected the twelve inches of upper-floor ledge she stood on, because one wrong move, and she would have been in midair, calculating the hardness of her skull against the acceleration of gravity. And since she'd already fallen, and had to climb the building again, she was especially careful of her footing.

What kind of person can love two people like that?

The kind of person who could love a killer, I decided, as I sat in front of Daniel, and Katrina closed the door behind me. I was the kind of person who was rotten inside, whose very core was drawn to the ambitions of others, no matter its form.

"The last time you came to me, at WDE, you said it was my last chance," I said.

"I did. And nice to see you, too."

"I said I'd ruin you, Daniel, and I meant it."

He smiled. I found myself disarmed by it. It wasn't a political smile but something more genuine that I remembered from the very beginning of our relationship, when he was starting as a prosecutor. That was before he'd been beaten down and had to be built back up.

"No, actually, you didn't mean it," he said. "You and I, see, we're in this tension. You got me in the palm of your hand, but I have you in my pocket."

"Really? Interesting. Tell me." I settled into the chair, swinging it so the back was to the computer screens. I betrayed nothing.

He said nothing immediately but looked me up and down as if considering something he hadn't seen before. "You look good."

"Thank you."

"Different." He put his hand out, cupping me in space. "I noticed it last time, but I was so thrown by you showing up I couldn't pin it down."

"I'm the same. Maybe the eyes that see me are different."

"No, not that, but maybe something else. You were always… I don't know the word."

"Do try," I said. "We spent so much time talking about how you looked and how you came across, so now it's my turn. I'm curious."

"By outward appearance, you're the same. Aloof. Ladylike. Perfect."

"And inside?"

"Feral," he said.

"If you'd known that earlier, things would have been a lot different."

He shrugged. "No way to tell. But, things have changed. And I'm not looking forward to this conversation the way you looked forward to the one you brought to me at the club."

"Oh, just get to it Daniel. Katrina needs her editing bay."

He nodded decisively as if changing gears. "I was thrown by our last conversation; I admit it. But I know you, and even if you've changed, well, I don't think you've changed that much. You're very protective. I know exactly what you have on me and how much it will hurt me. But if you send me down the river, I have enough on your little sleazebag to put him away. And you don't want that. I know he's got you around his finger. How he did it, I don't know. I thought you were with him to spite me, but I think I was wrong. He really has you."

"You have nothing on him, or you would have charged him already."

"I may. His accountant is running with Patalano now. If I catch Patalano, I have the accountant. Then I can get Spinelli. And guess what? He'll tell me whatever I want about whatever I want, in order to save you."

"Me?" I said.

"You."

"What—?"

"The attempted murder of Scott Mabat. Did you forget that? Scott hasn't. Because I traced the financing of this little picture right here." He indicated the room, the computer, all Katrina's work. "Big chunk led to him. So after we saw Katrina, we went to him. He didn't look too good. And I have to say, once I heard him tell his story, I didn't want to believe it. I didn't even want to think about it."

I swallowed. I'd known the gun wasn't loaded, but who would believe it? My face tingled, and I tightened my grip on the arms of the chair. I wasn't going to react. I knew how to do that. I knew how to present whatever emotion I needed to, and in this case, I needed to project confidence. I knew Daniel. If I showed him a crack, he'd wedge himself into it. "You have the testimony of a known loan shark against mine?"

"By the time this is done, I'll have Patalano and Niccolò Ucci telling the same story."

"I dare you." I leveled my gaze at him, consciously relaxing my jaw muscles as if whatever strength I had took no effort whatsoever.

"What happened to you?" he asked. "Inside. Where is Tink? Where's the woman who wanted to do the right thing, the good thing?"

This was how an heiress became a criminal. First, she didn't want for money. She wanted only to be normal and good. She flew under the radar her whole life, making sure there was always someone next to her who shone brighter, talked faster, and laughed louder. Then the sun she circled shifted, and she became disoriented and dizzy from being thrown out of orbit. She bumped into a dark planet and broke, from the force of the impact, into millions of white-hot pieces, blasting apart into a firestorm of euphoria, a soundless roar of exultation in the vacuum of space.

Daniel, as if reading my thoughts, continued. "I don't even know you."

"You never did. But in all fairness, I didn't either."

"This exciting for you? Running with this crowd?"

"Was it exciting for you calling your mistress a dirty little slut? I'm going to assume it's a yes, for the sake of my point. It all comes from the same place. We can only pretend we're clean inside for so long before we crack, and the darkness starts spilling out. You fucked her because you had to, to stay sane. I'm with Antonio because it's the only sane choice. I'd go crazy if I had to go back to who I was."

He leaned back, fixed his tie, and crossed his legs again. "I don't want to send you to jail. I know you think I don't care, but it would break my heart to hurt you. I have to try one last time."

"Try what?"

"To save you."

The screensavers on the computers went out, bathing us in a false daytime darkness. Feathers of light fell beneath the room-blackening shades.

"In a few weeks, there's a wedding," he said. "It's at the Downtown Gate Club. Is he taking you?"

"No."

"Don't lie, Tink."

"He's not."

"Make sure he does. I want you to be there on time. Wear your best gun-moll dress. During the cocktail hour, I want you to pass something to the bathroom attendant." He put a small manila envelope on the desk.

"You're a damn member, Daniel. Can't you give it to her yourself?" I said.

"They're going to sweep it before the place settings are laid out. IDs checked. Everyone's frisked for wires. And there's a mole on my team. I can't let it leak."

"What makes you think I won't tell Antonio?"

"I expect you to, and I expect him to stay quiet to protect you. Everyone's walking out in one piece. You're going to put an object in the tip tray, and you and your lover will ride into the sunset, for whatever that's worth. If you don't pass it, I'm having both of you prosecuted. And there will be no witness protection for you. You don't know enough to be worth it to the Fed."

I rocked in the chair, my eyes getting accustomed to the lack of light. I was in a terrible position, and I knew that. I had internalized my situation quite nicely in less than thirty seconds, because I knew Daniel. I knew when he was serious and when he was bluffing. It had been my job to know for too long, and it was a job I had a hard time quitting.

"I think I always knew you were like this," I said. "When we were together, I had a feeling that once I stopped being useful to you, I'd lose you. I think that's why I always tried to be a part of what was most important to you. I told myself I did it because I enjoyed it, and to a large extent, that was true."

"You never lost me. This is business."

"I never had you. I made myself a part of your career because I knew that if I didn't, you'd find a woman who would. So I'm going to tell you something about Antonio. I'm not useful to him. He wants me as far away from his business as possible. Maybe I enrich his life. Maybe I drag him down. I don't know, because I don't know what love is anymore. I only know that no man has ever loved me like he does. If love is part of our better natures, he's a saint. And if it's part of our basest instincts, he's an animal."

He sat still in his chair, hands on the arms, as the hard drives behind me wound down with a *whirr*. Then he smirked.

"You his Madonna ? Or his whore?"

I smirked back. The question didn't offend me, which was why I could answer honestly.

"Yes."

chapter 27.

ANTONIO

Barnsdall Park was a perfect private place. It was an outdoor setting yet private in its expansiveness, with crannies of bushes and low walls and a sheer drop onto Hollywood Boulevard. It would have been difficult, if not impossible, for anyone to casually listen to my call. I sat on the ledge overlooking the city as the sunrise bled red over the hills.

"Antonio," said my father, "*Come stai?*" In the background was the sound of Neapolitan traffic. He must have been in the city.

"Good, Pop. How are you?" I spoke in Italian, but my mind had always been elastic with language, and I knew I'd stumbled on my native tongue.

"You have an American accent," he said. To him, I sounded American. To Americans, I sounded pure dago. I was a citizen of that in-between place where no one would accept me as one of their own anymore.

"It's been a long time," I said.

"You sounded American in the first five minutes." He went behind a door, or closed the window, because the white noise stopped as if cut off at the knees.

"It's an efficient language. Easy to learn. You should try it."

"Sounds too German. All this *chop chop chop*."

"Well, it's good for fast decisions," I said.

"And bad for small talk, son. You didn't call to chat about phonetics. Not at this hour of the morning. What time is it over there?"

"Almost seven."

"Did you leave her in the bed alone?"

That made me smile. "It's almost like we're related. You and I."

We sat inside a pause. I watched the light traffic on Hollywood Boulevard, and he let me.

"I heard Donna Maria won't have Paulie Patalano in her family," I said. "She doesn't think he'd be strong enough."

"News travels fast when there are women involved."

"And she's looking for another match for Irene, because she knows the Bortolusis will crush her."

"There's only one match, son," he said.

"With Valentina, you took care of all of it. You brought me in. I said I'd give my life to the camorra. I let you make my decisions for me in exchange for vengeance."

"You said there would never be another woman. I believed you. I figured, he's my son. I know how he is." Regret coiled around his voice. "If I don't make this match, we're going to be crushed."

"I want out," I said.

"If anyone else questioned me, they'd be in the hospital asking forgiveness."

"I won't do it."

"They all say that. Your sister said it, then she fell in love with him."

"Then she was raped to prevent the marriage. Do you think any of this makes sense? Do you think we should maybe stop this?" I couldn't sit still. I jumped off the concrete wall and paced the jogging track, keeping my eyes off the horizon and focused on my feet.

"There's more American in you than the accent," he admonished. "This is not your choice. Not after the first one."

"These decisions were mine. And this one is mine, too. I'll do it with you or without you. With you is simpler."

"It's too late, Tonio. You gave up your life." He was angry, growling at me in a way he'd had no chance to do when I was a kid. "I told you this when you were my *consigliere*. I warned you it was the worst decision you'd make. And when you left my side to go over there, chasing them, I told you then, too."

"I'll sell the businesses. Peel off territory. Stop taking tributes. Just tell me what I have to do to get out."

"Nothing. You don't get to go back; that's the end of it. If you don't care about your own life, at least think about the woman. The one you're fucking. They'll kill her same as the last one who got in the way of business."

Stupido. God, that poor kid. Donna Maria killed his girlfriend, without a word of remorse for it.

"I know you think you can protect her," Benito said. "But know this. They'll kill you first then her. There's no message if she lives. And don't make a mistake. There are a lot of them. If they want you dead, you will die."

"How, then? How do I do it?"

"Don't let them smell weakness, son. If you want to out, you have to find your way. Don't whisper a word, even to me. I will try and stop you."

I watched the blood of the sun pour onto the city and knew that, years before, I'd sold my hopes in the name of vengeance.

"*Capito*," I said.

"*Bene,*" he replied. "After the Bortolusi wedding, you and I will discuss your courtship. It will be very traditional. You're lucky. She's a nice-looking girl. It could have gone much worse for you."

I rubbed my face. I'd never been less attracted to a woman in my life. I hung up without telling him that.

I drove up the mountain and through the flatness of the valley, up into the freeway split of the Angeles National Forest, where a man could be alone with his thoughts.

I didn't blame my father for what he was doing. I'd taken a *camorrista* vow to be at the service of the family. The camorra worked the way it worked because marriage was a business deal. My father was the result of such a marriage, so why should it have been different for me? The fact that he'd never been forced to marry was the result of luck. There had been neither necessity nor opportunity.

I drove faster. I had no business doing it. I was endangering everyone else on the road, but the faster I drove, the faster I thought. The other cars, and the mountains on either side, faded into a blur.

Benito Racossi, my father, counted me lucky with Valentina. I'd married the woman I wanted to marry. She had been outside the life, and I was finishing law school. My father was proud and grateful. My mother had even spoken to him for fifteen minutes without a fight.

I pulled onto an exit that wasn't an exit. It was no more than a bastard turnoff onto a dirt road. No gas stations, no fast food, just the potential for a city. It was a space set aside for something, someday. The freeway turned pencil thin in my rear view, and up ahead, the mountains went from shapes against the sky to solid masses of green and brown. I'd hoped to drive into a wall, but it didn't work that way. I knew that from home. The roads to Vesuvio twisted and rose gently until ears popped and the car slowed, but in increments. Halfway up the mountain, I'd realize I'd made a choice to go there.

And Nella, sweet Nella, my sister. Raised outside the camorra, she was promised to a man against her will then fell in love with him anyway. Like animals, a rival family gang-raped her to prevent the marriage.

cd reiss

I thought about what might happen to Theresa if I refused to marry Irene. That stupid man and his girlfriend had washed up on the sand because they'd refused.

But he'd been weak. What if I wasn't? What if I started with Donna Maria and killed every single son of a whore beneath her until I had what I wanted?

No. Even if I was successful, I'd be more deeply trapped in the life than ever, and Theresa might not survive it. I had to do better.

I pulled the car over and looked east. Indeed, I'd gone halfway up the Angeles mountains without feeling it. I looked out over the washed-out colors of civilization, the gas stations and fast food joints, and the stucco houses and dots of cars. They looked like plastic debris caught on a slowly heaving sea of dirt and dry grass.

I felt as if the world reorganized around the *camorristi,* spinning up and away. We nailed our feet to the ground with spikes of tradition while the whipping winds of modernity threatened to rip our bodies off at the ankles. And if it succeeded? If we let ourselves be yanked into the air? We'd fly and fly and be unable to walk when we came down, crippled by our fear of change.

I couldn't murder my way out of it.

I couldn't walk away. I was hobbled.

But maybe, just maybe, I could run.

202

chapter 28.

THERESA

Daniel's envelope had a set of seven flaccid wire lengths with plastic nodules on top, and it took me a second to identify them as earpieces. I was about to call Antonio. I wasn't going to keep a word Daniel said secret. I owed him nothing, and I owed my Capo everything.

I went to the Spanish house on the hill. The door was locked, and the Mas was parked out front. I went around to the side, where I could hear Puccini through the leaded glass windows. I called his name over and over but got no reply. Finally, the obvious occurred to me, and I texted.

—Capo? I'm outside—

The music went off. I waited, but he didn't come out. I went to the front of the house and found him by my car, driver's side open. A plume of smoke curled from his perfect lips.

He was smoking. That never boded well. He never lit a cigarette when everything was all right.

"You need to go," he said when I was within earshot.

"I have things to tell you." Did he hear I'd been in the same room with Daniel again? That wasn't my fault, and if that was the source of his anger, he was going to get an earful about waiting to talk to me before making assumptions.

"I'm sorry," he said. "Just go."

"Whatever it is—"

His face was stone cold. His mouth was set so hard the last wisps of smoke came from his nose.

I crossed my arms. "What?"

"It's not you—"

"It's you. I know. I've heard it. And I agree. It is you. It's all you. I'd be at work now, pushing numbers and fighting through protocol meetings, if it wasn't about you. So, what's this about now?"

He dropped his cigarette to the ground and stomped it out. "I'm leaving."

"I'm coming."

"You can't."

"Like hell," I said.

"I have two choices. I leave quietly, and I'll be hunted the rest of my life until they find me and kill me. Or I kill everyone who demands the marriage, and I protect you at the same time. Those are the two. There is no third."

"Another consolidation, to match the marriage in December."

I must have surprised him with my immediate understanding and my lack of emotion about it.

"Yes," he said.

"What century is this? Don't do it. Just say no."

"The last man who said no washed up on a beach with his girlfriend."

"The girl's going to get a complex."

"I'm sorry, Contessa. I'm willing to die. I'm willing to say no and leave the life, even though one day they'll kill me. But I keep thinking no matter what I do, I hurt you. And *that* I'm not willing to do. If I go away, and I'm not around anymore... sure, they find me. I don't care. Eternity is a long time. Another fifty years on this earth isn't much, by comparison. But, without you, it's wasted."

"And that's your plan? Run away and get killed to protect me?"

"I'm not dragging you down anymore."

"I thought the only way out was through."

"Don't ever doubt I cared for you," he said.

He walked back to the house. As soon as he walked back through that door, he'd be gone. He'd close the door and lock it. Then I could text all I wanted; I could call and I could come with a battering ram and a police warrant, but he'd be gone.

I ran ahead of him, wedging myself in the doorframe.

"One more time," I said. "Then I'll let you go. I'll never see you again. But one more time."

He was on me so fast I didn't have a chance to put my bag down. His lips crashed into mine, his arms cocooned me, and my knees came out from under me.

He shut the door behind me and pushed me with his lips and his intentions. I pulled his jacket off, and he undid my hair. His face an inch from mine, his palms on my cheeks, he kissed me, and in that kiss there was more love than I thought a human heart could contain.

"I want you right now. Right here. One more time for the rest of our lives." He kissed me with a mix of gentleness and depth. "Just a moment with you." His words were breaths made of desperation and heat. "Please. Indulgence. Saintly indulgence before the devil finds me."

It couldn't have been that cut and dried: marry another woman and live; stay with me and die. It couldn't have been that simple. But his mood wasn't nuanced; he needed me. There was no use denying it. Practical matters would have to wait.

"Take me." I raised myself. "How do you say it?"

"*Fammi tua.*" Even as he said the words, his hands were already up my shirt, feeling under the side of my bra and where the underwire creased the soft flesh. I turned and put my arms around him.

"*Adesso.*" He pushed his hardness against me, and I swung a leg over his waist to get him closer to home.

"*Fammi tua.*"

His hands crept up my skirt into my panties, finding the split in me, following the wetness.

"*Fammi tua!*" I cried. "God, is it my pronunciation? "*Fammi tua!*"

"You are my heaven." He hoisted me up, leaning me against the rock of his dick. "I can't say no to salvation."

He carried me upstairs, kissing me, and laid me on the bed. A full suitcase fell onto the floor, spilling everything.

He pulled his pants off. God, that piece of meat between his legs was a beautiful sight, and when he pulled his shirt off, the shape of his body looked built to fit into mine, every curve and line angled as if calculated to match to my desire.

Where was I going? What life was I living, without him? I'd be an empty shell of a woman.

He fell on top of me, yanking my clothes off until we were naked together.

"Wait." I pushed him away.

"I will not be told what to do."

He looked at me with such intensity that I knew he wasn't talking about me telling him to wait.

I laid my hands on his neck. "Daniel found me today."

"That son of a whore... if he touches you..."

"He wants me to go to the wedding and pass the bathroom attendant a bunch of bugging devices. He'll hurt you if I don't do what he says."

"I'll be gone. Dead, probably."

This man was willing to die rather than live without me. I wanted to save him, but maybe I'd be damning myself if I told him the extent of Daniel's manipulation. Even the fact that I was willing to use my safety as a bargaining chip made me wonder about my motives. "He'll file charges against me."

"You're not compelled to pass listening devices around, Theresa."

"The attempted murder of Scott Mabat. The loan shark."

His breath was deep and sharp. "When I murder Paulie, it will be for that."

"You said you wouldn't," I said.

But he would; I knew that. If he wasn't protecting a relationship with me, and the opportunity arose, he wouldn't hesitate to kill Paulie.

"I don't know what to do," he said as if admitting to a crippling weakness he'd hidden his whole life.

"Yes, you do." I brushed my hand against his cheek.

"I don't. There's no solution."

"There's always a solution."

He just shook his head. He believed it. He'd done the math and come up with the best, most selfless solution he could. Walk away.

"Fight, Antonio. Fight for me."

"I am fighting for you," he said.

"Fight harder."

He whispered it back to me. "Fight harder." Then he smirked, shaking his head a little. "Of course. I'll die fighting for a life with you. If they kill me for it, my fate is set. I'm marked for hell. I'm damned, and once this life is over, we're separated for eternity. So while I'm on this earth, every second I have is yours."

"And my seconds and my minutes and hours are yours. Will you take them?"

"I am yours, Contessa." He kissed my breasts and belly. "*Solo tua.*"

The particular strain of his voice, hinted with both intensity and hopelessness, gave me pause. But it was a short pause because his tongue was between my legs, finding ridges and edges, working around my core and then upward, tickling my clit.

He came up to me, face to face, leaving me still wanting his tongue. He hitched my hips up and slid his dick into me. "Forever. Everything I do with you is forever."

"Wait. A second. Wait. Just. Ahh." He fucked me so hard every thought went out of my head. He fucked the brains out of me, the common sense, the grounded quality he loved so much. I was gone. Every thread of maturity, wisdom, and care was gone.

I'd been his long before that moment. He owned me the first time he put his body on mine, since the first thrash of violence on my behalf. He'd owned me the minute he wanted me, even before I wanted him.

But it wasn't until he spoke to me in vulnerability, until I heard panic, until he came to me with nothing, that I owned him.

It was only at that moment that his salvation came under my care, and I became responsible for my own destruction.

chapter 29.

THERESA

We planned our annihilation like two chess players in the park, both hitting the clock after each move, thinking and rethinking assumptions, motivations, and methods. He was brilliant, and with each passing day, in my bed or his, we spoke of things no one should speak of and avoided any talk of failure.

Failure was death. And our deaths would mark our success.

It was one thing to agree to live with someone, to settle on committing to sickness and health, good times and bad, and to promise to live until living was no longer possible. It was a completely different thing to promise to die with them. And that was what we agreed to.

Antonio Spinelli and Theresa Drazen, two people from opposite sides of the world, with barely a language in common, whose bodies fit together like modular forms, were going to die.

The decision to die came at the end of a series of decisions. The first was to be together. The second was to fight together. The third was to leave together. The rest followed from there, because even before Hemingway, all good stories that were carried to their inevitable conclusion ended in death.

Our story would end in the death of Daniel's pursuit, of Paulie's threats, and of Antonio's status as a slave to his life. It would end in the death to my relationship with my family, my friendships, and my access to a few million in trust. All of it.

And most days, I was elated about erasing my past. How many people can start fresh with nothing on their backs? It was bliss to sit in serious talks with Antonio, even sprawled on the bed with a sheen of sweat, stained in his love, mind clear enough to think of some dirty nuance that needed to be managed.

"Daniel is still a beneficiary on my life insurance."

"Does it matter?" His mouth was taking my nipple in small bites.

It didn't matter because I had enough wealth already, and because it was too late to change the paperwork. It only bothered me because I didn't want Daniel to have my money.

"No, I guess not." I was stretched out, naked, on my bed.

"I'm supposed to meet my future wife the day after the wedding."

"A date?"

"Chaperoned, of course," he said.

"God, I hate this. I hate how I feel. I'm actually jealous of this poor girl."

"I'm going to stand her up by dying. That would make me the second promised Neapolitan in a row. Maybe she'll marry Paulie after all."

He handed me a little blue booklet: my passport. We'd agreed to die around the time of the Bortolusi wedding. We'd made plans for after our deaths, but still hadn't decided on how we would die, how our bodies would appear to be obliterated, or how we would slip away.

I flipped the passport open. The pages felt real, with crisp paper in multicolored shades. There were even some stamps in it already. In my picture, I looked optimistic and clean, like a middle-school teacher travelling on Christmas break.

"I have mixed feelings about the name," I said, tossing my fake passport on the bedspread.

"Persephone? The goddess of the death?" He kissed me from above, hands on either side of my waist, his upper lip pressing against my lower.

"She was abducted into hell."

"She kept running into the wrong types of men." He kissed between my breasts, moving the St. Christopher medal aside with his teeth. I put my arms around him, letting him move above me like the shifting sky. "And poor you, with only me at your feet."

He moved his lips over my belly and hips, and I over his, until our mouths could worship each other properly.

chapter 30.

ANTONIO

She understood. I thought she wouldn't. I thought she'd dismiss how serious our power and our traditions were. But she was from an old-fashioned family. I don't think I realized that until Thanksgiving.

"I want you to come," she said over the phone as I stood in the driveway, watching Zo go over building plans with his workers. Someday the house would be done, even if I never lived in it. "Thanksgiving is important here."

"I can't."

"I want you to come. That should be enough."

"No. It's that simple."

I couldn't believe we found the time to argue about something so mundane. It felt like practice for real life.

"I'm not some kid looking to show you off. I want you to meet these people. They're important to me. Do you understand what I'm saying?"

I did. And maybe I didn't want to go for just that reason. "I want to talk about this when you're in front of me and I can occupy your mouth with something besides your demands."

"Don't avoid this," she said.

"*Ti amo*, Contessa."

"I'll text you the address. I expect you there."

I'd found myself in the position of trying to talk her out of our escape plan. She would be better off without me. And I tried to convince her, but only wound up fucking her. I tried to slip away, but she caught me by my dick and had me.

I'd promised to protect her. It was a promise I realized I couldn't keep. I felt resigned to the difficulty of the path and also to the potential of it. The trick to dying without dying was to make arrangements without making arrangements. The strategy was to not break up, to not stay together, to not *change*. And the question I'd pose to her when she was in front of me would be, "Would I go to Thanksgiving dinner with your family under different circumstances?" I didn't think I would. Not yet.

"This has to be done," my father said over the phone as I opened the door to the basement. Lorenzo and I clattered down the wood stairs.

"I understand." Zo handed me a box of handguns. I had an armory under the house that had been moved from *l'uovo*. I had the phone tucked between my shoulder and ear as I pointed to one of the guns and mouthed the word *ammo*.

"She's a nice girl," my father said. "You've met her?"

"Yeah."

I chose the one thing I'd need: a small handgun, built for a woman's hand but large enough to stop a man. Zo took a box off a shelf and shook it. Full.

"When this is done, I want you back here. This is going to put a lot of vendettas to rest. You and Irene will be safe."

What was the answer? What would it be if I were going to live past the next few weeks?

"No," I said taking the box from Zo and heading upstairs. "I'm not going back."

You didn't say no to Benito Racossi. You said yes, boss. But I wouldn't have said yes. I would have said no and gone to Napoli anyway.

"Is this about *la rossa*?" he asked.

"Yes."

"Bring her."

"She's American, Pop. It doesn't work like that here." I pocketed the weapon and put the rest away, and we clattered back up the stairs. Zo shut the light and closed the basement door behind me.

"It's all right. I'll figure it out," I said. The conversation with my father was such a play. I felt like an actor reading lines.

"You always do, son. You always do."

I didn't think he knew what was going on, but he was suspicious. I could hear it. We hung up soon after. Zo put the box of bullets on the kitchen counter.

"Who's this for?" Zo asked.

"Wedding gift."

"Nice. She's hot, you know? You gonna, you know, get to know her better?"

"After the Bortolusi wedding."

"What are you going to do with the rich one?" He opened the little gun, popping the clip.

I shrugged. "She can stay around if she wants. I can handle two. What are you doing?"

"Loading it."

I took the gun away and put it back on the counter. I knew all too well what Theresa was capable of, even with an empty gun.

"I need a favor from you," I said. "If something happens to me, I want you to watch after Theresa."

"Why would something happen to you?" Zo was never the most fruitful tree in the orchard.

"I'm the last one. And if I don't take this Irene girl, Bortolusi doesn't have any real competition. Donna Maria's going to have to handle it herself, along with Paulie and the other camorra bosses who spend more time fighting than making money."

"Well, nothing's gonna happen to you."

"Well, if something does, you take care of Theresa, or I will come back from the dead and make you a very sorry man."

"In that case…"

"I trust you, Lorenzo. I want you to know that. Next to Paulie, you were the guy I trusted most."

"Paulie didn't work out so good."

"So, don't fail me. Don't fail me."

I didn't mean to be fatalistic, but it was hard not to be. There would come a time when the father I'd just hung up with, who I hadn't known the first decade of my life and who'd always had my best interests at heart, despite everything, would write me off as dead. And the friend here, in front of me, who was building and rebuilding my life, would be unreachable.

I was making the project seem easy to Theresa, and it wasn't. That decision was going to break her heart before it healed her.

"Something going on, Spin? Something you can tell me?"

"Yeah, and I think I need your help. I can't do it by myself. But I need to trust you. You need to take this to the grave."

"Okay." He seemed unsure.

I snapped a drawer open and took out a knife.

"No, no, no. Come on man…"

I cut the web between my left thumb and forefinger, drawing blood.

"Give it here," I said, holding my right hand out. Zo gave me his hand, and I cut it. We shook with our left hands, a mirror image of gentle society.

"On *San Gianni*, do you swear silence?" I asked.

"I swear it on the five stars of the river."

I let his hand go and yanked off a paper towel.

"You cut deep," he said. "What the fuck?"

"*Forza*, my friend. You're going to need it." I unrolled a towel for myself. I felt relieved to have his help. I couldn't prepare the way without him, because there were two paths. Theresa and I needed out path secured, even though it would never be tread. And I needed another path. It needed to be a separate one, yet connected at the beginning, with props and plans and a clear way for me, and me alone.

Because she wouldn't be coming with me.

chapter 31.

THERESA

We ended up at Sheila's most holidays. She had the children, and apparently their schedules held places in the pantheon. The Goddess Tina of the Late Naps needed a sacrifice, as did Evan, God of the Special Diet, and Kalle, Goddess of I Will Only Go Wee In My Own Pink Princess Bathroom.

It was easiest to just go to into Palos Verdes. Anyone who couldn't make it just didn't make it. It was impossible to herd eight siblings anyway, even if Daddy had tacitly agreed to be someplace else for a business function.

RPV, as it was called, was set deeply west and south on the map, and was practically inaccessible by more than one freeway, making it unmanageable for even the richest commuter with an actual job. A famous movie director's wife had started her own RPV-based Montessori school in her basement just to avoid having to bring her equally famous children to the Montessori school over the hills. Sheila described it as strictly a matter of geographical convenience. The children within a two-mile radius joined in, walking to school in packs and creating a true neighborhood enclave of a type that had once been the American norm, but with more money involved than most people would see in seven lifetimes.

Sheila answered the door, her more-blonde-than-red hair disheveled, cut into a bob, and her flip-flops showing off a weeks-old pedicure. She didn't even say "hello" when I was beset by children whose red-topped heads bobbed and swayed like the flames of birthday candles.

"Did you bring wine?" Sheila asked when I got through the door. Tina had latched onto my leg and insisted on being carried on my foot.

I handed my sister the bottle, and she snapped it from me with one hand while picking an oatmeal-crusted plastic spoon off the floor with the other.

"The turkey didn't make it." Her Pilates-toned ass worked the yoga pants as we walked toward the kitchen. "I'm having one brought in." Sheila's voice rose and fell in a childlike singsong, often ending sentences in a question. But underneath that sweet exterior rolled incredible rage. Pushed the wrong way, she reacted with blinding, illogical anger. So she didn't let much get to her anymore, or she'd lose control.

"What happened?" I asked.

"Dog got it." She swung her hand as if it didn't matter. "The mess was anthemic."

"Anthemic?"

"Like an anthem. It's the new 'epic.' Only Jon's here so far. Alma?" She turned to her helper, barking instructions in Spanish. The kitchen was indeed a mess, but without the usual holiday smell of good cooking. Just the food. All product, no process.

I heard men outside and saw Jonathan with David. My brother was instructing his nephew on the proper windup for some pitch, using an orange as a prop. The kid pitched it into the yard. I slid the door open.

Jon picked another orange off the tree and lobbed it to David. "You're opening your hips too soon, so you're getting zero power from the lower half of your body."

"Hey," I said. "Whatcha doing?"

"Basics. Again," David said, winding up.

"Wait, wait. This whole thing is in the hips. That's why you kick your leg. So don't forget to turn them."

David wound up and pitched into a tree about fifty feet away. The orange smacked against the trunk, bouncing off and landing in a pile of half-green oranges collecting on the grass.

"That's in the stands. You just took out Jack Nicholson. He's going to sue your ass."

"See, it's because you're making me turn my hips like that," David protested. He was ten and a funny kid, sixty-five pounds soaked in saltwater.

"It is not," Jon said.

"David." I sat at the table. "Your uncle knows."

He rolled his eyes so hard his brain should have been in his line of sight.

"Here." Jonathan poked him in the arm. "Watch."

He pulled another orange off the tree and pitched it into the tree trunk. It landed three feet below David's, even though its velocity had been much less.

"You just gave up a double pitching like a pussy." David grumbled.

Jonathan laughed. He had infinite patience with David's crappy attitude and stunted attention span. "Get out of here, kid," he said. "Go play Minecraft."

David rolled his eyes again, bobbing his head as he skipped off. Jonathan threw himself into the chair beside me.

"Uncoachable, that kid. Just raw energy all wrapped in IQ points."

"I wonder if you'd be so patient with your own kids."

He shrugged, fondling a short glass of whiskey with nearly melted ice.

"Sorry," I said. "I shouldn't have brought it up."

"Nah, Jessica's miscarriage was a long time ago."

"I feel like you guys never recovered from that."

"We took each other for granted. That's what we never recovered from. And me, I'm over it entirely. She stopped taking me for granted fifteen minutes after she saw me with someone else. It's sad."

"Where is this someone else?" I asked.

"I should be asking you. Where's the guy you were trying to not ask about at lunch? The one who says… what was it? *Come vuoi tu?*"

I think I blushed. It was easy to talk about his ex-wife and their failed attempts at children. Talking about my beautiful Capo made my skin prickle.

"Working," I lied.

"On Thanksgiving? Talk about taking someone for granted."

"Oh, Jonathan. Do we need to get laid?"

He nearly choked on his whiskey, and I realized I'd never spoken like that around my brother. As innocent as the words were, the sentiment was not from the Theresa he knew.

"Okay, okay!" He held his hand up in surrender. "I'll lay off the guy."

"Which guy?" Sheila asked from the other side of the screen door. Before I could answer, she continued, stepping back. "This guy?"

Beautiful even from behind a screen, Antonio stood, smiling and holding a bottle of wine. Sheila slapped the door open. I think I must have been smiling right back at him.

"Napa, again?"

"It's from Campania." He handed it to Sheila, who stared at him a second, smiled, swallowed. Antonio jerked his thumb inside the house. "The rest of the case is by the door."

"You brought a case?" Sheila asked.

"Theresa said to bring wine."

Sheila didn't say anything, but turned on her heel and went back inside. I was stunned. I hadn't seen Sheila blown back by a man in a long, long time.

"Antonio," I said, "this is my brother, Jonathan."

He handed it to Sheila, who stared at him a second, smiled, and then went back into the house. I was stunned. I hadn't seen Sheila blown back by a man in a long, long time.

"Antonio, this is my brother, Jonathan."

They shook and exchanged how-do-you-dos. Daniel had been the last strange man I'd brought to a holiday function, and he'd melted into the scenery as if he belonged there. But I wasn't worried about Antonio. There were so many men and women, friends and others, who came to Sheila's dinners, that Antonio's presence would be noted but not focused on.

"So, Theresa's told me all about you," Jonathan said.

"Really?" Antonio said.

"No, actually, not a damn thing."

"Don't mind him," I said to Antonio. "He's got all my worst qualities."

Antonio folded his napkin in front of him. "Then you must be a shrewd yet reckless man."

"You aren't describing my sister. You can't be."

"You're implying I'm not shrewd?" I said in mock consternation.

"I'm implying that, for you, a four-inch heel is reckless," Jonathan said.

The doorbell rang, and the chaos began.

chapter 32.

ANTONIO

I couldn't count all the adults at the house, much less the children, who were more restrained and more present than the kids in Napoli. I didn't trip over them. They were both more self-possessed than kids from home and wilder. They were shrewd with adults and seemed unable to negotiate their own squabbles or feed themselves. But I was so busy trying to remember names and faces of the adults that I didn't have time to give the children any of my reserves of memory.

I remembered Deirdre but pretended I didn't. I shook hands with Fiona and Margie and made a point of remembering them because they were siblings. Men came and went; there were boyfriends and husbands, and some were half a relationship I didn't understand.

"Thank you," Theresa whispered to me between conversations and questions I didn't want to answer.

"For you? The world."

"How are you holding up?" she asked as we walked the edge of the property where it fell to the beach. Beneath us, the waves crashed against the rocks.

"Which one is your mother?"

"My mother isn't here yet."

"Margie still looks at me like she doesn't approve."

"She doesn't approve of much," she said.

"I bet her husband is an unhappy man. Which one is he?"

"Doesn't have one."

"Too bad," I said. Our hands swung together as we walked along the property, leisurely heading back toward the house. We were still too far from anyone for eavesdropping, and the water made a good mask for our conversation.

"I'm thinking you need to come to the Bortolusi wedding," I said.

"How's that going to work while your father negotiates the value of your cock with the Sicilians?"

"You took on this dirty language with both fists, didn't you?"

"There's no other word to use. Does it bother you?" she asked.

"It makes me have to keep myself from taking you by the hair and putting you on your knees."

"Quick. Change the subject."

"If you come, it looks like a strategic move. It looks like I can walk any time, or that I want to."

"Keeping your frenemies on their toes," she said.

"Exactly." We'd gotten close to the house.

"Shall I ask for olive oil with the bread?"

Just as we came in from the patio, there was a crash from the kitchen, the volume and length indicating a mishap of some scope. It barely paused the conversations around us.

"None of the women are going to the kitchen to help?" I asked.

"She has a staff, but I was just thinking…"

Jonathan came up behind Theresa with his whiskey drained to the ice. "She kicked me out," he said.

"Does she need help?" Theresa asked.

"Would she admit it?"

She looked up at me. "Sheila might kick Jonathan out, but from me, she'll take help."

"*Andiamo.*"

"Jonathan, can you take care of Antonio? Make sure he doesn't step on a toe."

"Mom's not even here yet," Jonathan said.

She play punched him in the arm and went to the kitchen to see what had happened.

I tried not to look at her bottom when she walked away. She never swayed it or asked for attention with it, but her posture was so straight and proud, the result of such effort to remove sex from her gestures, that I got hard just looking at her.

But her brother was right next to me, and looking at his sister as if she was naked wouldn't make me a friend. I didn't know what future I had with Theresa, but I was sure getting kicked out of her sister's house at Thanksgiving wasn't going to help.

"You're the only boy," I said to Jonathan. "Of how many?"

"Eight."

"Protecting all these women. Sounds like a full-time job."

"You have a sister, then?" His Italian was accented, but fluid and nuanced. I had to remember not to underestimate him.

"Back home," I said. "Just one, two years older than me."

"She know everything about everything?"

"But, of course. How I breathe without her help, I always wonder."

He glanced around. I knew the look. He was seeing if anyone was listening. At least one of them must have spoken Italian. "Even after you came here looking for those *bastardi*?"

"Yes."

Though the shift in the conversation hadn't caused half a second of pause, and our faces betrayed nothing, it was as audible to me as a magazine clicking into place.

"Heard you missed one," he said.

"I haven't forgotten." I was being watched, indeed, by the redhead with the vapor cigarette and one of the men.

"Good."

"I think that's the only big failure in my dossier," I said.

Jonathan nodded. "We've decided to overlook it."

"No Italian!" Theresa had returned. She put her hand on my back. "Not fair. I don't know what you're saying."

"Did Sheila need anything?" Jonathan asked.

"Besides a mop? No. And she's letting the kids toast the s'mores before dinner."

They exchanged a look that seemed more intense than it needed to be.

"Oh, Jon don't tell this story," she said.

"Why not?"

"It's… I don't know. Inappropriate."

At the word, he took on a glint of mischief and leaned toward me. "Our dad took us to the club whenever Mom was unavailable, meaning *incapacitated*, and the nannies had the night off or were overwhelmed.

"Which was most of the time." Theresa was cutting in on the conversation despite her misgivings about appropriateness. "The 'overwhelmed' part, I mean."

"Yeah. Of course, he'd go off with his cronies to the Gate Bar to drink, and we'd be left in the TV room. Which had this big screen. At the time, this was a big deal."

"Oh, and movies on prerelease."

"Right. R rated, too. But mostly, we'd wander around, and at one point we got to the carriage house. It was me, Theresa, and Leanne, who was old enough to know better. But we saw these lights on and who knew, right? Maybe there were baskets of candy or some coke or something."

"We were too young for that."

"I think Leanne was dabbling. So. Hell, if there wasn't something going on. Out on the patio, it was so damn dark, but we smelled a barbecue and found it happening at the carriage house. A bag of marshmallows was right there. It was closed. The boxes of graham crackers and chocolate were, too. Leanne wouldn't let me have any unless there was no one inside. So we checked."

"How old were you?" I asked.

"Eight," he said. "By the way, it was the last time she got candy out of my hand. Anyway, so, you know, the carriage house was like a guesthouse for dignitaries, right on the Downtown Gate Club grounds. It had everything in it. A kitchen they never used, a little pool, and a sitting room, which we snuck into."

"It seemed like a good idea at the time," Theresa said.

"So, we're in there. And we hear this noise, like this slapping. And we're all curious. Oldest of us is what, eleven? And, get that look off your face," he said to me, "It's not what you think."

"It's ten times worse," Theresa said.

"We peek around to the living room, and then, I mean the slapping gets louder, and there's this…" He lowered his voice. "Woman, bent over the couch, with her bare bottom out, and a guy. Big hairy motherfucker of a beast, hitting her ass with a slab of meat."

I didn't say anything, because I hadn't heard that exact idiom before. But Theresa burst out laughing.

"I think it was a raw flank steak," she blurted out.

"Wait, what?"

"She covered my eyes. So sure, if she knows the cut of meat, I believe her."

"*Mio Dio*." I didn't even believe what I was hearing. I had to hold in an attack of laughter, because Theresa was taking over the story.

"The guy... he hears something, and he stops. We run. Leanne pulls us in some crazy direction—"

"She has no sense of direction. She gets lost putting her contacts in," said Jonathan.

"And we end up in the bedroom diving for a closet. We make it, but we hear the guy stomping down the hall, yelling in Russian."

"Czech," corrected Jonathan. "And I tell them, I whisper, 'You're my sisters, and I won't let him spank you with meat.'"

Though he'd kept his face straight until then, none of us could hold it in any longer. I laughed so hard I thought my guts would drop out of me. Theresa had tears streaming down her face, and Jonathan tried to finish the story between bouts of laughter. "Leanne, I mean she was horrified. She said, 'No one's spanking anyone with meat, Jon.' And then this one"—he pointed to Theresa—"says, 'he was just tenderizing it for the grill.'"

"I was protecting your eight-year-old mind!" Theresa said.

"Wait," I said. "You were talking? In the closet? Did he hear you?"

"We were in the tunnel by that time." Theresa wiped a tear away, then seeing what must have been a quizzical expression, she said, "There are moveable panels in the closet. All the kids knew about them. The carriage house used to be a speakeasy. There are tunnels under it that go across the street. From prohibition."

"Ah." I said. "So you got away?"

"Yeah," Theresa said. "There's one spot where it bent to a grate under the parking space outside, and if you stood one kid on top of the other, you could open it. I have no idea if those panels are still there. I'm sure they've been sealed during a renovation or something."

"They closed the connection between the carriage house and the grate," Jonathan said. "I was trying to lose my virginity a few years later and ran into a wall."

"It has to still be there," I said.

"It's all still there. Trust me. But the grate's not connected to the house any more. And that was the best escape route, too. Landed across Gate Avenue. Remember?"

"All right!" Sheila called out from the kitchen. "We're not waiting for Mom. So if you all want to eat, the caterer is here, and we're ready to go!"

chapter 33.

THERESA

We ate like kings and queens, princes and princesses. I didn't taste any of it. I was memorizing Leanne's slovenly ponytail, Sheila's lilting singsong, Margie's clipped wit, Deirdre's errant curl and sober scowl. Jonathan said nothing of importance, deftly avoiding any meaningful, personal subject matter as if he were in some sort of pain he didn't want discussed over dinner. I wanted to corner him and ask what was happening. But then he told some joke and got a witty rejoinder from Margie. He laughed. I smiled at my brother and wondered how I would make it through the rest of my life without hearing his laugh.

Antonio put his hand on my knee and squeezed it. I put mine on top of his, and we looked at each other. I felt a third hand on my knee. It was smaller, softer, and slick with grease.

"I wanna hold, too!" I peeked under the tablecloth. It was Kalle. She had a turkey leg in her hand and poultry bits all over the front of her sequined dress. She had a lump of Play-Doh in the other hand. It smelled of dry bread dough.

"Can you wash your hands first?"

"No! I don't like to wash my hands!" She left a big stinker of a three-year-old's handprint on Antonio's pant leg.

For some reason, when she giggled at the shape of the grease stain, a lump rose in my throat. I smiled through it and excused myself. I got myself together in the bathroom. I had to choose between my family and Antonio, and I loved this family, at least my siblings, but I didn't want to be without my Capo. Not for a month or a year. Too much of my life had ticked away while I'd been doing things that made me unhappy. I'd settled for the wrong choices, followed the wrong people, and betrayed myself for too long. I was doing what I wanted, no matter how much it hurt.

Sheila was waiting for me on the way out.

"Theresa? Are you all right?" Her lilt, as if she spoke to a hurt child, would have driven anyone else crazy. It might have had that effect on me, but at that moment, I needed it.

"This guy? He's not hurting your feelings is he? Because I'll be happy to rip his spine out." Even when making death threats, her voice was gentle as a lullaby.

"Him? No. He makes me very happy. I think I'm just tired, and I had too much wine."

I hugged her tightly. I couldn't let it go too long. I couldn't cry on her shoulder. If I did, she'd know something was wrong. But in my mind, I said goodbye to her and to all of them.

Antonio didn't ask me anything until the car ride back.

"Do you need to back out?" he asked. "I won't mind. I'll understand."

I ignored him. I knew I could back out. "Are you supposed to propose to this girl or something?"

He pressed his lips together as if he didn't want to answer. I waited.

"After the Bortolusi-Lei wedding."

"How soon after?"

"Very soon. There's all kinds of formalities. I have to ask Donna Maria first, then have chaperoned visits… and on and on. But they won't suffer the power imbalance too long."

"I think we should die at the wedding," I said. "I think everyone should see it. I mean there are easier ways, for sure, but they'll be questioned."

"What did you have in mind?" he asked.

"We don't need to just die," I said. "We need to be obliterated. Let me finish working it out, but I think the wedding is the place to do it."

He nodded, as if understanding the gravity of what I was saying. As if he saw me shaking, he said nothing more on the drive to the little Spanish house.

I had given no thought to death, unless I wanted to be paralyzed with fear. I was afraid of neither pain nor hell, but death? Death crippled me.

It was the thought of nonexistence that took my breath away. The idea—and it was only an idea—that we ceased completely was no comfort. I felt only terror, because I wondered what my life had been in the first place if my consciousness could be so utterly snuffed. And in those moments that I allowed myself to feel, and thus fear, my nonexistence, the shattering vulnerability of my corporeal self overtook me until my skin crawled at the thought.

Was my consciousness made of carbon and electrical impulses? And was I more than that consciousness, or less? Contemplating death made me question life. Consciousness was all that I valued, and if I ceased to think when I fell into that infinite sleep, what exactly was the living me?

I would go with him into death, into that deepest of vacuums. But our death would be special, a birth into a new life together. Everyone else had to go into blackness alone, to hold up the earth or to fuel a fire.

We just hadn't worked out how exactly we would die. And then, in the middle of the night, it came to me.

"Antonio," I whispered, turning and finding his eyes already open.

"Yes?"

I caressed his cheek with the backs of my fingers, and he kissed them.

"Fire and tunnels."

The answer was fire; that had never been in question. But there was always the matter of an escape route, and it came to me on the drive home on Thanksgiving.

The tunnels under the carriage house were part of a ten-acre system under downtown, built inside basements for deliveries, initially, then for drunken escapes from the underground speakeasies in the 1920s. Each block had its own network of basements and tunnels, and, in the case of the Gate Club, there were only two ways to get off the city block. The first was down the grate and across Gate Avenue to an unused trapdoor in a driveway; the second was the speakeasy way, through the carriage house, across Ludwig Street and into a residential basement.

The grate was in a small parking lot. We couldn't use it without being seen going down it, so that option was out. The carriage house had no cameras to protect the privacy of important people, and the walls were thick for the same reason. It was perfect.

"You drew this?" Antonio said when I handed him the map. He was freshly showered. His lashes looked darker and thicker, like black-widow legs.

"I wanted to get it right."

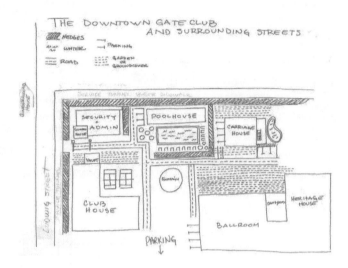

"You really do need a life."

I swatted him. "*Basta.*"

He cocked an eyebrow at me, and I pointed to the map. "Okay, this is the layout. As I remember it, the tunnels went from the carriage house, across Ludwig, into the gingerbread house. It's really long, but if we run…"

"And you want to blow up the house?" He said it as if it were a possibility, but it sounded absurd to my ears.

"Yes," I said, embracing the absurdity. I picked up a red marker and drew on the map.

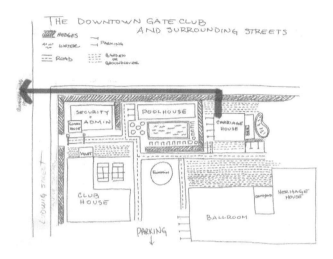

"Here to here. Done. The service tunnel is straight because they used it for deliveries."

"But there's another way?" he asked.

"Yes, but it's not connected to the house. There's a grate here. I don't know how we'd get to it without being seen."

He took the map from me, and the red pen, and drew his own lines, at one point plucking his own black pen from his pocket for an accompaniment. I loved watching him work, the concentration. I wanted to work with him, to see that part of him all the time.

"This is how it's going to go," he said. "According to you and your brother, there's a tunnel across Gate, not connected, and a grate we can't get to. But we can."

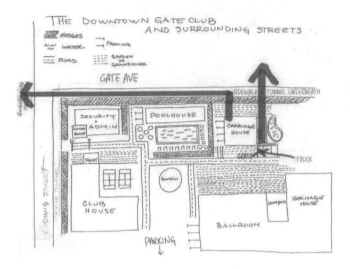

"How?" I asked. "The grate's right there. You can even see if from the ballroom if you just look through the trees."

He winked at me. "You check out the way across Ludwig, and I'll see what I can do about the short way."

chapter 34.

THERESA

I could go look at the carriage house, under the pretense of planning a stay there at some point after the Bortolusi wedding. I could even put a deposit on the place, as if I were expecting to be alive to throw an actual party on the grounds. But that would be a paper trail. It would be known that I went to look at the carriage house weeks before the wedding that was the scene of my death. And Daniel was blindly ambitious and emotionally void, but he was not stupid.

So, I had to look at the other side, and that was where I got lucky. The gingerbread house across Ludwig Street was for sale. It sat in a tiny residential enclave in the middle of downtown, protected by a Historic Overlay Zone.

A two-foot-high plastic A-frame sign sat by the streetlight, with the address written in chalk under the words "Open House!" Three white balloons had been tied to the corner with blue grosgrain ribbon. The breeze had twisted the ribbons into a stiff braid by the time I got there. I parked on the corner and walked as if I wanted to check out the block.

The houses sat close together. None were the same; none held to a stylistic similarity. The gingerbread house was the only one of its kind for miles around, with swooping peaks and dormers, shingles that curved over the edge of the roof, and a red door. Grey stone covered everything from the porch floor to the path leading to it. The windows were small, plentiful, and painted blue at the crosspieces.

The house had been staged in period-appropriate furnishings, except the kitchen, which had been redone in glass tile and stainless, probably to raise the sale price. Couples milled about, looking in closets and trying to find reasons to buy or not. They made notes and whispered, talking to each other about the real-estate market and its pattern of booms and busts. I smiled noncommittally at everyone and drifted between rooms. I opened the cabinet under the sink. It was filled with cardboard boxes. Whoever lived there hadn't moved out all the way yet.

"Hi there!" I turned, taking my hands off the knob as if I'd been caught peeking in a friend's medicine cabinet. In the doorway stood a woman with cornrows and a white smile, clutching a clipboard to her chest. "I'm Wendy! Did you sign in?"

"No." I smiled back. I intended to neither sign in nor explain why.

"Were you interested in the neighborhood, or gingerbread in general? Because we have another one in West Adams."

"Is it in the overlay?"

"It is."

"And the renovations here," I indicated the kitchen. "Approved by the historic district?"

"All the modernization by the previous owners was approved." Her smile hid something.

"And before that?"

"If you were planning to do any remodeling to the basement, there are some adjustments you'd need to make. We have a very rare basement in this house. It was modernized without approval ten years ago."

"Can you show me?"

"Us too," said a man who had been taking down the model number of the microwave.

Wendy perked up. She led us down a narrow stairway that twisted in the middle, down to media room with industrial carpeting, leather couches, and a screen that took up the entire space. One window set high in the wall looked out onto Ludwig Street. I touched the wall under it.

"This is a fully functioning media center, but as you know…" She nattered on about Historic Preservation Overlay Zones and districts, the rules that had to be abided, how her agency would help buyers navigate the process, and why the media room was still a great addition.

But I was thinking about tumbling into that same basement through the trapdoor, stinking of old dirt and

Fiona's cigarettes, falling face to face with an oil-heater tank. The basement back then had been dark as hell, with the only light coming from the moon through the street-level windows. I'd navigated piles of fabrics teeming from boxes, an old gas grill, and a plastic Christmas tree with light strings still on it.

I lost myself in the memory of that near-illegal thing, running my hand over the wall where the oil tank had been set. It could have been defined as breaking and entering, maybe. I hadn't been elated or paralyzed, but had entered a zone where my senses tingled, and I focused on one thing only: getting out. I calculated the time, the distance back across the street, the likelihood everyone upstairs was asleep. I checked out the window to see if the car was in the drive and wondered if I could climb through it without looking like a burglar.

That had been the only time I'd crossed the length of the tunnel to the house on the other side, and the gritty trip back to the club had been uneventful. But I poked the memory to see what had changed, and just about everything had.

I looked at the one remaining window then down. The wall beneath it was solid, and cool to the touch, as if stone through and through. The panel to the carriage house tunnel had been bricked over. The tunnel out was a dead end, literally and figuratively.

We'd have to figure something else out. The tunnel was blocked, and we couldn't use the grate exit.

—Where are you?—

I didn't know if I'd ever get used to Antonio just demanding my location, but knowing we were in a special circumstance, I tamped down the offense and went outside to call him.

"I'm looking at a house," I said. He'd know what I meant.

In the background, I heard sirens and men shouting.

"Are you all right?" I asked.

"I'm fine."

"What are the sirens?" It wasn't unusual to hear sirens in the background when someone called from outside, but they'd never caused my chest to tighten and my breath to shorten before.

"Don't get in your car. Otto will come for you."

I didn't ask. He wouldn't tell me over the phone.

As if he'd been nearby the whole time, Otto showed up ten minutes later with a half-eaten sandwich in his lap.

"Hey, Miss Drazen. You have the beemer?" He opened the door for me.

"It's down the block. What happened?"

"The blue Mas is gone. Pieces of it are still falling outta the sky."

"What?"

"Car bomb."

"Is he all right?" I asked, even though I knew he must have been, or he wouldn't have called.

"Everyone's fine. Spin caught a bit of shrapnel in the leg. The thing went off when he unlocked it. I'm telling you, that shop has taken a beating. They gotta start over."

"Who did it?"

"We got our ideas." He said no more.

chapter 35.

ANTONIO

I never saw the bomb that went off in Napoli, the one that had my wife declared dead. It had been a column of smoke over the mountains. Then, when Zo met me halfway down the mountain to tell me what had happened, I didn't breathe until I saw the circle of black and the carcass of the car.

The bomb in Los Angeles was so different I didn't make the connection right away.

The shop had just come back to life and was populated with men hauling wood, wielding nail guns, and shouting to each other. They'd gone to the Korean pizzeria for lunch, leaving tools behind and work undone, but the garage had been reframed already.

When I unlocked the Mas as I was heading toward it, my mind was on Theresa and how she'd fare without her family. I doubted she'd make it, yet I had to believe she would. I was thinking I needed to choose whether to believe she could stay by her word or to doubt her when the car hopped as if animated. The motion was barely visible, and the tires never left the earth, but only became more circular at the bottom, losing the weight that flattened them to the ground.

I only had time to kiss the ground, as if I'd kicked my own legs from under me. The sound deafened me, blasting the top of my head, velocity of the air pushing me back an inch or more, and a rain of glass followed for the next sixty seconds.

I spent that entire minute convincing myself to breathe, because I'd never been that close to a car bomb.

My life was getting simpler and simpler. I was being pushed through my options one by one until I had none left. Seemingly all at once, I'd gone from having a few enemies and a couple of soured relationships to being a target.

The forensics unit was in the process of clearing every scrap of glass and metal; every speck of carbon and dust went into a bag. I was treated like a criminal, not like a victim, even when I sat outside the back of an ambulance. I was questioned for an hour about my whereabouts that morning (Zia Giovanna's, which was verified) as if I'd blown up my car for the insurance money. Once they realized who I was, the tone of the questioning changed. My shop was cordoned off with yellow tape, and the contractors were questioned. I knew they'd walk away untroubled and come back the next day. They were my men. If they weren't trustworthy, they wouldn't work for me.

I went through the questioning before an EMT saw the blood on my trouser leg and pulled me into the ambulance, sitting me down as if I couldn't do it myself. She was insightful and gentle, with a straight brown ponytail I might have taken a try at pulling in the past.

"What kind of car was it?" she asked while she cut my pant leg, her plastic gloves wrinkling at the knuckles.

"A Maserati Gran Turismo."

"This year's?" She spread the pant leg open. A piece of metal was lodged in the muscle of my calf.

"Last year's. I liked it too much to get a new one."

"Nostalgia. I get it. This is going to hurt, Mr. Spinelli." She squirted the wound with a blue liquid that stung nicely. But I knew that wasn't what she was talking about.

"This your shop?" She didn't look me in the eye. She was pretty, even as she held onto the metal with a pair of sterile pliers. Carefully, she pulled the metal out of the muscle. It did indeed hurt.

"Yeah. Past five years or so."

"Looks like it's taken a beating."

"Rough month," I said. She pulled out the last of it, holding it up for me to see.

"The car was blue, huh?"

"Custom paint."

She plunked the metal into a tray. "Nice." She squirted the green liquid to clean the wound. It wasn't that bad. The expectation of pain was always worse than the actual thing.

"Looks pretty good," she said, peeling the skin away, looking for debris, and squeezing her liquid in the crevices. "I can take you to the hospital if you're worried about scarring."

"Scars are the proof we've lived."

She looked up at me. "You're going to have a really nice bit of proof here."

I took my cigarettes out. I needed one. Not for the gash in my leg. I didn't care about that. But the bomb made a good impression as a message. The bomb was a flexed muscle, a chambered bullet, teeth that were bared and ready to rip a throat. But only if necessary. Next time I wouldn't be so lucky, in theory. That was what I told the police.

I leaned my head against the side of the truck and let the pretty EMT clean my leg. I wondered what the hell I was doing, and why. Money? Power? My vengeance was complete. I had nothing. My family was an ocean away. I had no partner. My business was burned down. I wasn't the lawyer I'd wanted to be. I had no future outside of a beautiful woman who would tire of my secrecy soon enough. I wished I'd been inches from that car, because I was exhausted from running, from hunting, and from keeping secrets.

Otto pulled up across the street, and my Contessa got out before the Lincoln had even come to a full stop. She was my hope, that woman, standing so straight as she crossed the street. She could rule the world. She already ruled me.

chapter 36.

THERESA

We didn't say anything to each other when I saw him in that ambulance. We didn't need to. I sat next to him and held his hand. He waved Otto away. The EMT put bandages on him without a word, other than instructions on dressing his wound the next day. Then she left to take care of someone else.

"Those were nice pants," I said.

"I have more."

"Who did this? Paulie?"

He shook his head, leaning it on the side of the truck. "No. The Sicilians are watching him. This was the Bortolusis. I'm the last *camorrista* prince. If I'm gone, there's no merger."

"And you're going to the wedding? I think I should forbid it."

"It'll be the safest place in the world on that day. Paulie's been too quiet, and it's you he wants."

"That's our last day on earth."

He squeezed my hand. "*Si*."

"When you leave, there's going to be a power vacuum. Paulie's going to try and fill it. I'm thinking I have a couple of days to plant a seed in Daniel's head about him. Just put him on a trail. That'll get my ex off of thinking about where our bodies went, and Paulie will be preoccupied with sworn statements and such."

He huffed a short laugh. "My God. You have the heart of a capo, do you know that? You could have brought Sicily to its knees. No don would stand against you."

"I'll call Dan tomorrow."

"No." He squeezed my hand when he said it. "Make an appointment for the day after the wedding. Say you have something on Paulie. Say you're checking it out."

He seemed so melancholy, so much a swirling black pool of sadness, that I was drawn in with him.

"Can I take you home to the loft and feed you soup?"

"Ah, Contessa, I have to—"

I stood. "You have to nothing. Get the hell up, Capo." I held my hand out, and he clasped my wrist.

"No don could stand against you." He smiled as I hoisted him then grimaced when he leaned on the leg.

"You need to lean on me?"

"No. I'm all right."

"Antonio."

"Yes?" he said.

"Next time you do something like this, you need to tell me first. I was worried. I don't want to panic like that again."

He stopped and faced me, a smile playing on his lips. "Are you saying I blew up a Maserati? My favorite car? To what, set a pattern? To get the next one to look just as real? Come on, that car cost a hundred thousand dollars."

I crossed my arms. "All of Zo's guys are gone. He always leaves one to sit with the tools. He eats lunch out the back of the truck, but not today."

"Contessa, even if I had done such a crazy thing, I wouldn't have told you. You'd try and stop me and get yourself hurt."

"One day, you'll see me as a partner, not a responsibility."

He put his arm around my shoulder, and we walked back to my car, his bloody pant leg flapping against his calf as he tried to hide the fact that he was limping.

chapter 37.

THERESA

I laid him out on my couch and fed him minestrone I'd poured from a can and heated in the microwave. He complained about the saltiness, demanding I try Zia Giovanna's the next time I was there. "When she makes it, you can taste everything. This, I don't even know what's in it." He took the bowl from me and put it on the side table then pulled me on top of him.

"What are you going to do about Zia Giovanna?"

"How do you mean?" he asked.

"Daniel's taking those books, and I don't know if I caught everything. He's going to have your accountant. He won't prosecute an old woman. That would be political suicide. But the restaurant?"

He pressed his lips together into a fine line. "Without me, she'll go back to Napoli with her sister."

"Come on, Antonio—"

"Not everything needs to be controlled. There are no formal charges against her. She can go any time. It's like you. No charges in the thing with the Armenian. If I were gone, he'd drop it."

He was dead wrong, about Zia Giovanna at least, and I didn't know if he was lying to himself or just to me.

"I had a thought," I said.

"Another one?" He stroked my hair.

"Greece," I said.

"I don't speak Greek." He pulled my shirt up and slid his fingers under my bra, the tips bending my nipples.

"Weather's nice. Government's totally corrupt." I groaned at the trilling sensation between my legs. I pushed myself down on his erection. "After we bounce around. When we've erased everything. We can settle there. Fuck on the beach every day."

He got my shirt and bra off in one movement. "That would be nice."

"Nice?" I unzipped him.

"*Simpatico.*"

"That's better, Capo."

I stood up and wiggled out of my pants, naked before him in seconds. He held his hand out, and I took it, putting a knee beside him.

"*Tu sei preziosa per me.*"

"I have no idea what that means."

"*Io ti farò del male per proteggerti.*"

I straddled him, putting his dick against my wetness. "Nothing. You get nothing until you translate."

"You think this stupid wound will keep me from taking you?"

"*Fammi tua,*" I said into his ear.

"Your accent is terrible."

I slid myself against him. "*Fammi tua.*"

"To save the world from your Italian, I'll tell you what I said. It was, 'I'm going to fuck you easy and slow, until your bones turn into jelly, and you forget how to beg me.'"

"When? I want you to fuck me. Please."

He moved my hips and shifted until a sharp upward stroke was all that he needed to impale me. I gasped. He grabbed my ass cheeks and pushed deep into me until I felt the pressure inside.

"Is this what you want?"

"Yes."

He rocked against me, his body rubbing my clit, and I threw my head back.

"Like this?" he asked.

"Faster."

"Faster what?"

"Please."

"*Per favore,*" he said.

"Oh, no. I can't."

He stopped moving and smiled an evil grin, brown eyes glittering. "Say it so I can hear it."

"*Per favore.* I want it."

"*Lo voglio.*"

"*Lo voglio, Capo.*"

I leaned forward, and he gathered me in his arms, holding me close and controlling my movement. "*Sei così preziosa per me.*" He whispered it over and over as the heat between us built to a red throb, slowly, in a rhythm that went from pleasant to tortuous without changing.

"Wait for me," he sighed.

"*Per favore,*" I cried. "Faster, please."

"Wait for me."

I nodded but had no words until he said, "*Sì.*"

He held me to the rhythm, and I felt every step of my orgasm: the foothills, the climb to the mountain, and then the volcano dripping lava as I cried for him. My face pressed to his, my mouth opened wordlessly, and he put his lips to my tears and came into me, clutching me as if he'd never let me go.

chapter 38.

THERESA

I lived in an unreality where my life was marked in days. And having made that absurd, stupid choice to end my life, I lost my mind.

Antonio was shrewder than I was. He wanted to leave everything alone and let it sort itself out. I wanted to leave a neat little world behind me, where everyone could be happy. Anything less seemed cruel. I kept twisting contingencies around in my mind, trying to find the best and worst outcomes and to fix all I could without raising flags. What damage could be prevented? Was there a single favor I could call in and never repay?

There was.

I didn't tell Antonio. We'd be long gone and he could be pissed at me as we fucked on a beach on a Greek island. The thought of a rabid hatefuck on a beach made me smile, in public, on an elevator to the

Century City penthouse, where ODRSN Enterprises had its offices.

"Daddy," I said when he turned the corner and entered the bright, sparkling reception area. My father was in his sixties. He still stood straight at six foot four, wearing a four-thousand-dollar suit and a face still handsome enough to turn heads.

"Theresa." He handed a folder to a tall, blonde receptionist. She slipped behind the glass desk and answered the phone, smiling like a robot. My father had impoverished the family trust. Then Jonathan had rebuilt it and sold it back to J. Declan Drazen. Since then, my father had been a businessman worthy of the original Irish-born Jonathan O'Drassen and just as bad a parent as the Irishman.

"What brings you out here?" he asked.

"Looking for a job."

"Really?"

"No."

He laughed and led me into the corner office. The windows were on a slant, as if it were a greenhouse where all the plants had been removed and replaced by an expansive desk and maps of Los Angeles everywhere.

"I'm glad you came by." He indicated a leather chair and sat in the seat next to it. "I've been meaning to talk to you since Thanksgiving."

"It's my turn to say, 'really?'"

"Tell me first, how are you doing since you left WDE?"

"Fine. I've been working a little on my friend's film."

He leaned back. The leather of the sofa squeaked. "It's not like my daughter Theresa to not have any plans. Fiona, yes. Leanne, sometimes, but you? You always were very sensible."

"It's not like I need money to live."

"You never wanted to live on your trust."

"I'm just in between things."

He shook his head slowly.

"You don't approve?" I said.

"You're all past my approval. Which is too bad. But no, since you asked, I don't. I heard about this man you took to Sheila's?"

"And?"

"Is he the reason you quit your job with nowhere to land?"

The visit had been a mistake. He did what he always did: he took control of the conversation and made me uncomfortable before I'd even gotten to the reason for my visit. And he'd do it until I either blurted out what I wanted or left without mentioning it. He had that way of interacting. He just wanted to make us squirm. He wanted to take the rug out from under us. It was his *way,* and even when he'd been called out on it, he'd laughed. Only Margie could manage him, God bless her and God fuck her.

"I quit my job because I was miserable. I have nowhere to land because I hadn't set anything up. I hadn't even thought about it. I've spent my whole life inside a sensible little box. I got tired of it."

"So you went 'outside the box'? That's very cliché, Theresa. I'd say you're better than that, but you're not a creative soul. I thought you were at peace with that."

His tone was so gentle and sincere that his words didn't sound insulting. I knew they were, but he wasn't trying to offend me, so I took no offense. He had a way of cutting deep without letting a person put up a defense.

"I am, but I've been thinking about what to do, anyway. There's a trust I need released to my discretion. There's only one left that you still have control over."

"I know the one. What were your plans?"

His interest was piqued. He knew I didn't want to pack it up my nose or blow it on the ponies.

"Antonio's aunt has a restaurant in San Pedro. It's being investigated for fraud, and I've looked at the books. It's clean, but broke. He can't help or he'll be accused of laundering money through it. He's pulled out completely. She's a nice old woman. The restaurant is all she has. I want to help her."

"How nice of you." He didn't believe a word of it, or at the very least, he didn't care.

"And because I know nothing is free with you," I said, letting the first part of the sentence sink in. He nodded. He didn't care what any of us thought of him. "I can donate half to the Wilshire Golfer's Club. I can finance a renovation. I think the carriage house could use a touch-up?"

He waved my suggestion away. "They haven't done anything in eighteen years. They won't fix that thing until an earthquake flattens it, and it's already survived two."

"You name it, then."

"For this man? This mobster?"

"For me," I said.

He looked out the wall of windows. "Have you ever wondered how I have so many children and so few grandchildren?"

"There's Sheila."

"She can't make up for the lot of you. Margie's a spinster. Carrie is off somewhere. Fiona, thank God..." He rubbed his eyes with a thumb and forefinger, as if truly troubled. "It's the men you girls choose. I don't know where you find them."

I could have made a crack about the example he set, but to what end? He was too old to change, and I was too old to take what he said personally.

"I'll tell you what," he said, taking his fingers from his eyes. "Make a good choice, one good choice, and I'll release the funds."

"Define a good choice."

"Whatever this phase is, finish it. Go back to who you are. Start making sense again. Then go back to Daniel. I'm sure he's apologized. Am I right?"

"Dad, really? What will this solve?"

I shook my head. This was a waste of time. Dad had done his share of philandering, enough to put him and Mom on opposite sides of the house. I should have expected that kind of old-world nonsense.

"Is this business?" I asked. "Are you looking to have the mayor in the family?"

"I know what makes sense when I see it. That's all."

He did, and Daniel and I had always made sense, always been perfect on paper, and that was how Dad saw everything. He never understood actual human emotion, which was how we ended up having a conversation with him thinking the ridiculous was possible.

"Just think about it," he said. "My insistence might be a favor in the end."

"I will."

When I stood, I saw a picture on a shelf, a big one of the ten of us at the Santa Barbara campground, each in our own world. Margie looked more a sister to Mom than a daughter. Jonathan, at twelve, was already bursting with puberty. Fiona's hair was tangled. And there I was in a button down shirt and lace collar, chin up, skin without pimple or blemish from sheer force of will.

"This was the year after," I said, stopping in my tracks.

"After what?"

"The boy."

"Which one?"

"The one at the bottom of a ditch," I said.

"Yes?"

"I went through middle and high school convinced you did it."

He held up his palms, one finger still wrapped in a ring that didn't mean what it had decades before.

ruin.

"These hands are clean," he said and denied it no
further.

chapter 39.

THERESA

"I need your phone," Antonio said, standing over me in a jacket and trousers. I'd grabbed his pillow and pressed it to my face, breathing in his burned-pine smell.

"Why?" I grumbled into the pillow. Why was I so relaxed in that happy limbo between living and dying?

"Because I need to put a detonator in it."

It was a normal weekday-morning conversation. It wasn't even exciting or titillating, but right and real in a way nothing in my life had been before. I shuffled around in my bag and handed him the phone. He took it and pulled me to him, pressing my nakedness against his clothes.

"You have a call from your sister," he said, holding the glass to face me.

"Of course I do. She must be scolding me about something."

The text came up first.

—Jon is at Sequoia. Heart attack.
Looking at a bypass where the fuck
are you?—

My hand covered my mouth. I'd ignored my phone because nothing seemed as important as what we were doing, but Jon at the hospital? I hadn't expected that.

Antonio held his hand out for the phone. "What is it?"

"He's thirty-two."

"Who?" He looked at the text.

"I have to go see my brother." I stepped away and headed for my pile of clothes. I had no intention of bathing or delaying another second. Antonio just stood in the middle of the room, my phone in his palm.

"We should call this off," he said.

"Let me see what it is first."

"You love your family."

"Antonio!" I shouted. I hadn't meant to shout. "Just let me go see him, okay? Then we can decide."

***

Sequoia took up a few city blocks on the west side, the hub of a medical community with research centers for spokes and uniform and equipment suppliers at the outer rings.

I found Jonathan sitting on the edge of his bed with tubes all over him. He looked drained of everything but frustration. Sheila sat in the chair by the window, tapping on her phone like she wanted to poke through it. Under stress, the rage came out.

"Hi," I said, kissing his cheek. "You look good."

"He wants to get out of here," Sheila said.

"They're holding me until I'm stable," he growled. "And I'm feeling more unstable every hour."

"What happened?" I asked. "You're hardly old enough for this."

"Can I not review this again?" he said.

"Honestly," Sheila said, all the singsong gone. "It's just his youthful indiscretions catching up with him. But if you make him tell the story again, he's going to chew your face off, and it's not worth it. He needs a bypass. He's going to get it. End."

"They do them during their lunch hour. It's just which lunch hour that's the question." He laid back. I sat in the chair next to the bed. A tray sat next to him with a plastic container that was empty but for a piece of cut pineapple.

"They're letting you eat pineapple?" I asked.

He looked at me as if I were crazy then followed my gaze to the container. "That's Monica's."

"Where is she?" I asked. "Is this is the new girl?"

"She comes at night," Jonathan said.

"Mom thinks she's a gold digger taking advantage of Jonathan's infirmity," Sheila piped in. "So she comes at night, and we avoid the drama."

"That's ridiculous," I said, pointing at Jonathan. "How can you do that to her? Do you love her or not?"

"She doesn't need the aggravation. Believe me."

I shouldn't have cared about some girl I'd never met. I shouldn't have cared about one of my brother's dalliances. But he was so young and so sick, and I was disappearing in a short time; I felt as if the smallest problems were dire, and that if I had one tiny bit of wisdom to offer him, I owed it to him because it would be the last.

"Commit, Jonathan. Just commit."

I walked out a couple of hours later, after laughing and crying with them, knowing I'd take my own advice to heart.

chapter 40.

THERESA

I felt as if I were studying for a test. We drilled day in and day out. We drilled in the shower and in the bed. He fucked me and wouldn't let me come until I got all the answers right. He still had my phone, so I called Jonathan from his phone. My brother invariably growled at me because he wanted to be out making money or bedding the new girl. Then Antonio would begin again as soon as I hung up. He was a rough taskmaster, demanding perfection.

How is it going to go, Contessa? Say it again.

First thing, I deliver the earpieces to the bathroom attendant. I come back. During the cocktail hour, before they introduce the bride and groom, I go outside.

Why?

I'm meeting you for a fuck. There's a florist's truck in the parking space over the grate. The florists are setting up the ballroom. I go in. The florist is owned by a business associate. You made the truck and sold it to them. I go in the false bottom. You have left a brick of C4 and a handheld crowbar under the chassis.

What else?

Guns.

What am I doing then?

Asking Donna Maria permission to marry her granddaughter.

Then what?

I wait for you.

Wait for me, Contessa, no matter what you think you hear. No matter how long you think it's taking. I'll be there. We'll run across the street and blow up the truck.

And there will be two explosions, because C4 explodes twice.

In the chaos, we come from the grate in the street and get in the car.

What kind of car is it?

A Porsche.

Perfect. No one would believe it was you.

Do you have it?

I have it.

chapter 41.

THERESA

It wasn't my wedding. I wasn't wearing white. I didn't have bridesmaids or an excited family. I hadn't chosen the venue or the catering, but in a way, I was coming out of the event a woman entangled with a man to the death. We were committed, tied in ropes of lies and deceit, each able to destroy the other if we escaped the net.

I wore a short grey dress with matte silver-bugle beads. The looseness of the skirt made it easy to move in, with heels that were more comfortable than they looked. In my bag I had lipstick, credit cards, jewelry, and an obscene wad of cash. I'd memorized my account numbers and passwords for my overseas banks.

I heard Antonio come into the loft, downstairs.

We'd never discussed getting married. It was too soon, but with the intensity of our commitment, I wondered if we'd both been too busy with practicalities to bring it up or if we were simply scared of making it official.

He came behind me in a black tux that fit him without an errant crease or curve, brushing his fingertips on my arms. His touch was still perfect, still arousing, designed to bring my skin to life. He dropped my phone on the vanity.

"It's done," he said.

"I press the home key?"

"Yes. Three seconds. But wait for me. We can both detonate. If we're not together, one has a good chance of blowing the other up."

He kissed my bare shoulder and looked at me in the mirror. "You look like a queen."

"How do I taste?"

"Like a woman."

I shuddered, arching my neck until the back of my head was on his shoulder. "You didn't have this power over me three months ago."

"And you? You were just a figurine on television," he said.

I turned, put my arms around his neck, and pulled him to me. "A miserable one."

He cast his eyes down. "So many things could go wrong today."

"Nothing will go wrong."

"Wait for me. You have to wait for me."

"I'll wait in the tunnel under the car, I promise," I said.

"You don't come out until I'm there. Then we exit the tunnel together. I checked. It's open on the other side."

"Yes, boss," I whispered.

"*Ti amo*, Theresa. Please don't ever doubt that."

I kissed him because the doubt he forbade me was all over his voice. I knew he loved me, at that moment. I knew I had his heart and owned his soul. Today.

But maybe he was wondering about tomorrow. Something was off.

I didn't want to doubt our plans. I wanted to be on a plane to Greece as Persephone, goddess of the underworld, with my Adonis next to me.

"You have to know," he said, "I'll always take care of you. I'll always think of you first. You're precious to me."

"Can you get that suit off and show me?" I hiked my dress up to show him the terribly impractical garters I wore.

He looked at them with a ruefulness I didn't understand, drawing his finger around one of the legs and yanking it.

"Do you want to be late?"

"I don't see that it matters. Come on, Capo. I'm wet. You're hard. Give me that cock one last time before we die."

With a quick stroke, he ripped them, reducing them to tatters in seconds. He threw me onto the bed. "Open your legs," he said, undoing his belt. "Show me your pussy."

I bent my knees and spread them apart. My pussy cooled when the air hit it. I kept my eyes on Antonio and then on his cock as he pulled it out. "I love you, Capo."

He kneeled on the bed then licked his hand and pressed it between my legs, entering me with three fingers. "Wet to the death, my love."

He didn't make me beg but fucked me without preamble. I thought, as he drove into me, growling my name, wrinkling our good clothes, that this was the man I was fucking forever. I dug my fingers in his hair and said his name over and over until I could no longer form words.

chapter 42.

ANTONIO

I was a bad man. I knew that when I met her and when I stood at her door the night she called me *Capo* the first time. And I knew that when I came inside her on the day she planned to disappear with me.

She didn't know she wasn't going anywhere with me.

She was going to live. She was going to get over me and find herself a lawful man to take care of her and fuck her gently. She was going to have children who lived as citizens of decency, and I'd twist in hell, knowing that she'd mourn for a little while and then find happiness.

was about to open a work of art in a museum, and at early o'clock in the morning, I found myself curled up in front of a locked door, my mind going in circles.

In between those questions and stumbling blocks over my house, I had to ask myself if I wanted that man in my life. Due to my prolific musical output over the past Jonathan-free weeks, I knew he was a work-stoppage waiting to happen. He knew it. That was why he'd walked out in wet underwear rather than take me right on the floor.

I really did wish I hadn't touched him that first time. I wished I hadn't taken that monkey of a bet that night at Frontage. I wished I hadn't met him at the Loft Club after his trip to Korea, and I wished I hadn't forgiven him for kissing Jessica. I had had every opportunity to take control of my life, but I didn't.

I watched the sky go from navy to royal, to cyan, to baby boy blue. I'd entered a fugue state of regret and dissatisfaction but had found no sleep. It wasn't a good day to be tired, but I had to get up and do the work.

chapter 43.

THERESA

The club was not its usual self. A line of long black cars backed down the block as each driver and passenger was identified, cross-checked and let through. Or not.

Why was I nervous about going through? I felt as though I was about to star in a musical production where there would be no encore, no repeat performance, no ovation. And under those nerves was a lightness I could only describe as elation. I was leaving everything behind and starting fresh. The possibilities were endless and had been barely scraped by my imagination.

Antonio, driving a three-year-old Alfa Romeo, reached over and took my hand, knotting the fingers together in my lap. "You all right?"

"Yep."

"Wait for me." He inched forward in the line. "Remember."

"How do you say it in Italian?"

"*Aspettami*."

"Will you take me to Italy some time? My sister lives there."

He took his gaze off me, and turned in to the gate, stopping at the guard station.

"Well?" I asked.

"Yes. Sure." He squeezed my hand and let go.

"Hello, Sir," the guard said. He wore a boutonniere in his uniform, a little white carnation wrapped in green and fastened with a pearl-head straight pin. "Can I have your name?"

Another security guy took down Antonio's license plate number.

"Antonio Spinelli," he said.

"And you, ma'am?"

"Theresa Drazen."

"Can I see some ID?"

We showed him. He checked our photos and took the license numbers down.

"Romance in America," Antonio said, quietly joking.

"Movie stars and mobsters get the same treatment."

"In Italy, they'd just shoot anyone who made trouble. To avoid the war, you play nice."

"We're about to ruin the whole party," I said.

"We are mad, aren't we?"

"We are." I squeezed his hand. "Let's do this. Before I go to the truck, let's enjoy this. Let's forget

everything and dance for one hour. Let's be who we
could have been. Just Antonio and Theresa, with a real
future and boring pasts. I'll act like my biggest
problem is whether or not you like my dress. And
you'll act like yours is how to get under it. We'll be the
most thrilling things in each other's lives."

He touched my lip, turning it down, then stroked
my chin. "You already are the best thing I have."

"Pretend I'm also the worst thing."

"I haven't earned the life you just invented for
me."

"Mr. Spinelli?" The guard leaned down, our
licenses on a clipboard.

Antonio turned from me. "Yes?"

"Sorry about the wait." He handed the licenses
back to Antonio. "Can you get out of the car?"

"No problem."

We were frisked. My bag was rooted through.
They fingered the space behind my ears and looked
inside them with the same little handheld lights doctors
used, apologizing the whole time. Across the way, on
the line of cars coming the other direction, another
couple was getting the same treatment. Then the
guards smiled and nodded, letting us through as if
patting down guests was normal.

chapter 44.

ANTONIO

Was it wrong to give her good memories of me when I
knew I was leaving her? Yes, it was. I should have
been making her hate me. But if I was going to keep
two conflicting ideas in my mind at the same time, one
was going to sweeten the bitterness of the other.

I was being selfish, but her suggestion that we
enjoy the wedding appealed to me, and I couldn't let it
go. So after we gave the valet our keys and walked into
the Heritage House, I guided her with my hand at the
small of her back, which she relaxed into as if she
belonged there. When the champagne went around, I
took two glasses and gave her one, looking deeply into
her eyes when we toasted.

"Am I getting dirty looks?" she whispered to me.

"Not today."

If any part of our plan failed, by the next week,
she'd be the *camorrista* whore. But I'd be long gone,

and no shame would be brought to anyone. That day, to everyone but a few, she was just a woman I'd brought to a wedding.

"And Paulie's not coming? You're sure?"

"I'm sure," I said.

Donna Maria sat at a small cocktail table with Irene and Carlo, shaking hands with subjects who passed. Irene wore a blue shift dress that went to the floor. There was no sign of the hypersexed little flirt I'd seen in the yard. She avoided looking at me.

By the dais, Bernardo Lei and Giacomo Bortolusi, the fathers of the Neapolitan bride and Sicilian groom, respectively, held court as if this coronation were the end of years of competition, when in fact it was only the beginning.

"We have to go pay our respects," I whispered to Theresa.

"Can I get drunk first?"

I removed the empty champagne glass from her hand and led her to the line.

"I once met the Queen of England." Theresa said quietly.

"Really?"

"Elizabeth. My whole class went. It was a trip to London, and you know, private school. Los Angeles. Rich people, blah blah. I wasn't even nervous. And when it was my turn in line, and I said 'How do you do?' exactly like I was taught, I could tell she was just bored out of her mind." She tilted her head to the right slightly to see the front of the line, the curve of her neck begging to be touched and bitten and licked to a bruising. But I couldn't touch her. She turned back to me. "These guys don't look bored."

"This is the height of their lives. A business arrangement disguised as a marriage."

She squeezed my hand. "Have you ever thought of just doing it? Maybe it won't be so bad?"

"How could I go back to earth, having kissed heaven?"

I didn't know if I was leading her on. I wondered if speaking the truth to her in those last hours would just make the separation worse. Would it make the sting of her hurt be lengthier or go deeper? Would the venom course through her veins longer, or would she just have some honest piece of me to hold onto after I left?

"Master Racossi!" Bortolusi bellowed. He knew my father and was his main competition in the cigarette trade. He was ambitious, cruel, and ruthless.

"I go by my mother's name," I said as I shook his hand, looking him in the eye. I was famously unashamed of my bastard lineage, and I wouldn't take any shit about it.

And he knew it. That disconcerted me.

"This is Theresa Drazen," I said.

He took her hand and kissed it. She was perfectly gracious, neither too proud, nor coy, nor embarrassed.

"Pleasure to meet you," she said.

"I recognize that name."

"I have a big family. You might have met one of my sisters. I have six."

He laughed and nodded then turned back to me. There was a line of people behind me, waiting to meet the father of the bride, but he took the time to put his hand on my shoulder. "A little bird told me I'll be seeing you back home in a few weeks."

"You shouldn't listen to birds," I said. "They chirp what they hear, not what they know."

He laughed, but there was no humor in it. We shook hands with the gentle Bernardo Lei, who made no insinuations. Then we met the groom, who was boisterous, half drunk, half bald, and a bride who beamed with pride. Despite the reasons for the union, it looked like a good match.

"Shall we dance?" I asked. "I think we have time for one."

"He said you were going back to Italy? I thought you couldn't?"

"If this goes through, everything's forgiven. Come on, let's go dance. I'm not looking for absolution from anyone but you."

chapter 45.

THERESA

I was glad I didn't speak Italian. It meant I could smile through the half conversations and small talk Antonio endured on the way to the cocktail room. I didn't have to attach meaning to any of the looks I got. I only had to pay attention when he was addressed in English.

"*Consigliere*," an old woman said from a seat we passed. She wore a black dress and shoes, no makeup besides years of sun, and brown eyes sharp and clear.

"Donna, it's been years since I was your consul," he replied in English with a rote, joking tone, as if they'd been through this a hundred times.

"It still has a nice ring to it. I haven't met the lady."

I put my hand out. "Theresa Drazen. Lovely to meet you."

"Maria Carloni. I'm sure you've heard of me."

I swallowed. Smiled. Ran through my mental rolodex, cross referenced her with Daniel, in the subcategory 'nice things felons do.'

"Yes. Of course. The Catholic Woman's League."

She laughed in the way an old woman does when she can, because she's old and she doesn't give a shit what anyone thinks anymore.

A young woman in a modest blue dress handed Maria Carloni a drink. She was lovely, with olive skin and brown eyes the size of teacups.

"You've met my granddaughter, Irene, Mr. Spinelli?"

"I have." He took her hand and bowed a little. "Nice to see you again."

She didn't meet his gaze but curtseyed. Something in the gesture was formal, yet intimate, and I felt a surge of jealous rage I worked to cover with a noncommittal smile.

I wasn't introduced.

Antonio took my hand and pulled me away. But as fast as he got me away, I heard Irene mumble, '*puttana*,' under her breath. I was no scholar, but I knew what that meant.

Things had to be normal, right? I had to act like we were just walking out of here and going home and fucking. I had to act as if nothing had changed, and nothing ever would. I had to do things any typical woman would do on any particular day.

So I turned and smiled at her, then put my fingers to my lips and blew her a kiss.

"What are you doing?" Antonio asked.

"Being nice gets tiresome."

"Contessa."

"Yes, Capo?"

"You make a beautiful cat." He pulled me two steps toward the piano player. "But you're already dangerous when your claws don't show."

He turned me until I faced him. It was too early to dance, but he put his arms around my waist and pressed me against his body. I laid my fingers on the back of his neck.

"She's cute."

"I'm sure she fucks like a log in the woods."

I smiled. He had a way of saying the exact right thing.

"The flowers are beautiful," I said. "Did you see the truck? I saw it pull around to the Heritage House side."

"They're setting up the ballroom now. I made sure they were late."

"Bad, bad capo."

"It's what I do." The music stopped and people stood. "Ready?" he said. "We're moving over."

The party shifted to the Heritage Room, which I knew intimately. A big room that was part of a big building, with few doors and high ceilings gilded to the teeth. It was our last stop before we escaped this life. I reached for my phone.

"Who are you calling?"

"I didn't talk to Jonathan. And I'm…"

Dying.

I clutched the phone, trying to find the words for what I'd forgotten to do.

Antonio laid his hand over mine. "No, Contessa. Just leave it. I'm sorry. Come on. You were the one who wanted one dance. Let's have it."

He pulled me into the center of the room, which had been fashioned into an ad hoc dance floor. The band struck some tune from the eighties, a happy kickoff. We were the first ones on the floor.

He pushed my hips away with one hand and pulled me back to him with the other. We turned, stopped, and kicked together. I must have been smiling because I squeaked with delight when he turned me and smiled back. The world blurred outside our movements. It was only us, stealing a dance, a moment, the space around our bodies an indefinite haze that had no bearing on our coupling.

I forgot everything except the places where his body pressed to mine, and his skin touched my skin.

When it was over, the band didn't stop but went right into the next song. Antonio pulled me to him. "There are two more songs before they introduce the bride and groom. We're sitting them out."

"You're a good dancer," I said. "Wherever we go, let's make sure we dance."

He nodded. "We're here."

We sat at a round table with two other couples I didn't know. He greeted them in Italian, introduced me, and put his hand on my back when we sat. He glanced at his phone and cursed under his breath.

"It's early. The truck. They finished setting up the ballroom already."

"Let's go, then." I grabbed my bag.

"The doors are open. No one will see us go. It's pointless."

"I'll go then. I'll keep them there."

He put his hands between my knees, like a teenager who couldn't keep his hormones in check. "Go do what you have to do in the bathroom. Now."

"Why? I mean, who even cares if I do Daniel's bidding?"

"Trust me."

I squeezed his hand and stilled my heart long enough to look into his eyes. I was doing this for him and for us. I was doing it to be a different person and finally shed my skin of pretense.

I kissed his lips and stood.

"Okay, Capo. I'm going."

I carried myself, more than walked, to the bathroom, slipping in with my head held high. I gave my hair a quick swipe in the sitting room then went to the area with the sinks and the attendant.

Her chair was empty.

Of course it was. I was a good fifteen minutes early. I put on lipstick, smiling at two women who came in and snapped the stall doors shut behind them. A third woman in a pale-blue dress came in, coyly swaying her hips. She puckered at me, as if she expected me to be there.

"Hello, *puttana,*" she said.

"Everyone in America knows that word, Irene. You're not getting it past me."

The attendant came in. She looked vaguely Romanian. Her name pin said *Codruta*, and she did not make eye contact with me.

Irene blushed a little, shrugging. She played with her curls. I put on more lipstick, patting it with a cloth towel. When the two women in the stalls came out, I made room for them, but stayed by the sink. My hand was in my bag, around the tiny envelope, but I had no idea when I'd get to pass it over.

"He'll never marry you," Irene said when the two women were gone. "He'll always run away."

"I'll chase him."

"He's not keeping a whore when he's married to me."

"Then I hope you like anal sex."

Her look of abject horror was priceless. Codruta suppressed a laugh. I let mine out, chuckling and sliding my bag off the vanity. The bag got behind a stack of towels, and they fell to the floor like dying white butterflies.

"Oh, I'm so sorry!" I said.

"It's fine," Codruta said. I kneeled down to pick up the towels and slipped the envelope between two, handing the short stack to her. "I've got it, thank you." She looked at me pointedly, nodding ever so slightly and pressing the envelope's bulk between her fingers.

"You're welcome." Then, looking at Irene in the mirror, I said, "It's really very hot. You should try it."

That was cruel, but I couldn't have helped myself. Not one bit. I was only human, after all.

I walked out the door and through the cocktail hour as if onstage. Invisibility was not the objective. Antonio wasn't at his seat. I kept a noncommittal smile on my lips as if I were going for a pleasant screw in the back of a flower truck, and no more.

I don't know if, even at the height of my scandal with Daniel, I'd ever felt so exposed, so watched, so in need of the poise and control I'd been famous for. The goal, in both instances, was to be seen, noted, and found unthreatening.

A few stragglers wandered outside, mostly smokers and some younger girls in short dresses, discussing their makeup into their compacts, as if announcing the brand of their blush into a microphone. I paused until one of them saw me then glanced around as if looking for something.

Breathe, breathe, breathe.

The truck came into view. It turned out to be a van. Deep blue, with flowers bouncing around white clouds. A man got out of the driver's seat.

"Hi," I said. "Are you the florist for the Bortolusi wedding?"

"Yeah."

"The mother of the bride says the orchids on the dais smell."

"Smell?"

"I don't speak Italian, but it was something like toilet. She's pretty pissed."

He sighed and slammed the door. "Well, hell. Let me check."

I knew he wasn't going to be able to get near the mother of the bride until after the introductions. So all I had to do was get into the truck.

I thought I might hesitate, but I didn't have to. The truck windows were black with tint. The blue seemed more saturated than normal; the smooth coolness of the handle seemed sharper than the weather should allow. The click of the driver's-side door, as it opened, seemed loud enough to wake the dead.

It swung open easily. I got in and closed the door behind me with a *phup*.

New-car smell. Fragrant flowers. An Egg McMuffin. I slid into the back and lifted the carpet. Potting soil dropped like a waterfall, gathering in the crease. I peeked underneath. It was just like he'd said, a ring and a loop.

I could still hear the music of the second song. He'd come in less than five minutes. I'd be waiting, just like I was told. I yanked up the door.

There was engine stuff down there, just as I'd been promised. But somehow, enough space had been made for a slimmish man to get through. Past that was the drainage grate. It was smaller than I remembered. Or I was bigger, because everything about the iron circle looked the same.

Reaching down until my legs splayed above me, I found the box bolted under the floor and opened it. I found the micro crowbar and a gun. When I picked up the gun, I felt the weight of the bullets, and I swallowed. The situation was real. Very, very real.

The space for the C4 was occupied with a brick that looked like clay and smelled like Play-doh. Weird.

"They smell fine!" I heard from outside. Sounded like he was talking on the phone. "I don't know what she's on about."

"Fuck!" I whispered.

Should I get out and sit in the back as if I were waiting for my boyfriend to show up? Or get the job done and slip into the hole?

The voice got closer. I put the crowbar to the side of the grate and dug it between the dirt and the metal.

No. It was heavy. This had been Antonio's job. I was going to have to pull up, back into the truck and act like a horny woman at a wedding.

"Hey!" I froze. It was Antonio's voice from outside, followed by a mumble from someone. Then Antonio. "I don't know. She said it was the purple? And there are white? Go ask. Who the fuck knows?"

I wasn't big enough to do Antonio's job. The grate was too heavy, and my arm wasn't long enough. I got out from the trapdoor and put the micro crowbar and the gun into my purse. I heard footsteps on the asphalt. *That must be him. God bless him.*

I put my feet into the hole under the truck, and lowered them until they hit the grate. I wiggled, bent my knees a little, wiggled farther, prayed I didn't get stuck, and shifted until my knees were on the grass and my torso stuck out the bottom of the truck.

"God help me," I whispered as I picked up my arms and slid down. My dress stayed up and I was naked below the truck. "Ever the *puttana*," I grumbled, sliding down. My breasts caught on a tube or tank or something, and I shifted again.

I hoped Antonio would get there soon, if for no other reason than to laugh his head off.

I heard voices. One was Antonio, sharp and loud. The next I also recognized, but I didn't have time to have a feeling about it before the truck shook.

The truck shook again, and I heard something hit the ground outside.

Paulie: "Who's saying *Ave Maria* now?"

Antonio, with a grunt: "You are." *Bang. Shake.*

And then there was nothing.

The music started again from the Heritage House. People would start milling as the salads went around; then they'd sit. And I was here, half in and half out of a truck. I let my breath out and twisted, sliding, falling into the bottom of the truck as if it had given birth to me.

I looked back up and wondered if I should close the trap. We were supposed to be coming together, but Antonio was apparently dealing with Paulie, and I had no idea if he needed me or if staying put was the thing to do. The carriage house was twenty feet away. I could make it across to there from under the car without being seen. I couldn't hear anything from the car, and that concerned me more than anything.

Aspettami.

I was supposed to wait, but I was sure Paulie hadn't been anticipated, and I had no excuse to be on my belly, under a florist's truck. I'd figure something out. I'd told him I'd wait, and that meant he'd take whatever action he needed to with the assumption that I was going to be under the truck. I scooted back and got my fingers into the dirt at the edge of the grate. The leverage was better, and I could get it up and slide it over if I could get the micro bar under there.

The party picked up across the field. I could hear the music and shouts of laughter. But over that, I heard a *pop* from the carriage house, and that was it. Some reactionary hormone flooded my bloodstream. I wasn't lying there another second, waiting for the plan to get even more screwed up. Without thinking clearly, because all I could think was that everything was off, and Antonio was hurt, I scuttled from under the truck and ran to the carriage house in my heels, flattening my skirt at the same time. I was sure I was full of grass and mud. I was sure that I couldn't return to the party looking like that, but I was also sure Antonio and I weren't going back for a dance and aperitif.

The house was bathed in the flat light of sunset. I took three steps and cast a three-foot-long shadow over the grass. I flattened myself against the wall, listening. Stuff was getting thrown. Things were breaking. I trotted to a window, but it was obscured so I couldn't see in. Only out. Damn the privacy of the privileged.

The door sat inside a cut in the wall, and I slipped inside it. The knob didn't turn. It never did. Even when

I was a kid, the front door had been a joke, a double-reinforced barrier against an unknown enemy.

Fuck it.

I ran around to the back of the house. The patio looked the same as on the night Leanne and Jonathan and I had come across the uneaten steak-and-s'mores dinner. And like that night, the sliding door was open enough to get through.

Nothing had changed, but the dining room table was off kilter and a bunch of porcelain knickknacks were in pieces on the floor.

Not a sound came from another room. Not a crash or a scuff, or a word, and that concerned me. I was tempted to call out Antonio's name. I needed to know he was all right, that he was there, and to let him know I wasn't waiting under the grate.

But I didn't, and I think that saved my life, because as I approached the bedroom I heard a thud, and a breath, and the words in an exhausted gasp… "Too easy, motherfucker. That was too easy."

I should have run, but that hadn't been Antonio's voice. Tiptoeing, I peeked in then flattened my back against the wall. In that flash of a view, I saw Paulie, hunched, breathless, face bloody on one side, and a set of legs that only could have been Antonio's.

I had a gun.

He'd given it to me for a reason, and if that wasn't his intention, what was? I reached into my purse for it. Things clicked. My clothing rustled. It must have sounded like a klaxon in a morgue, because Paulie, who was not an idiot, and was as much of a killing machine as my lover, heard me and sprung into action.

I was an accountant. I paid attention to the machinations of money. My talents were on paper. I was not a specialist in the art of physical confrontation.

So, when Paulie snatched the bag away, I just stood there, stunned. And when he grabbed my arm and threw me against the bedroom wall I flew like a rag doll, smacking my head on the corner of a marble tabletop. My vision collapsed into shattered webs of light with blackness at the edges.

"Well, well," Paulie said. "What a sweet little present this asshole gave you."

My vision cleared to a pinpoint of clarity, with him at the center, my gun in one hand and my bag in the other. He dropped the bag on the floor.

The circle of clarity widened. I blinked. Tried to move. Paulie held the gun, checking it for bullets, popping the clip, slowly, as if he wasn't worried about a damn thing. The room swam a little when I moved my eyes away from him.

Antonio faced away from me, his head in a pool of blood. He wasn't moving.

Oh, fuckjesusmotherfuckerhell.

"I know you're pissed he was promised to Irene," Paulie said. "But to get him in here for a screw then shoot him? Man, you women are just nuts, you know that?"

I tried to say Antonio's name and failed. I got my feet under me and braced myself against the wall, which swam and rolled.

Paulie crouched on his haunches. "You want to do it yourself?" he asked. "He shelved you, you know. He'd keep you for a fuck, but he was marrying that girl, no matter what he told you." He dangled the gun in front of me. "You want to take this cheating asshole out?"

Past the gun, with my focus improving but confused, I saw Antonio's finger move. Just a twitch. Was it a death spasm? Some relic of life left in him? Or was it the result of an intention?

"I won't." I croaked.

"Man, you Drazens." He shook his head in mock pensiveness. "You got this badass rep. But, buncha rich pussies if you ask me."

My wits had returned. I glanced at the pile of crap on the floor, located my phone, and put my gaze back on him.

"Why are you alone, Paulie?" I asked. "No one love you anymore? Couldn't find an ally to take out an enemy with?"

He smirked. "In the end, it's on me." He grabbed my hand and put the gun in it. "And you, Princess." I yanked my hand away. He pulled his arm back and swiped the gun across the side of my face.

I think I flew. I think things fell and crashed, because a bolt of light followed the one that came from the impact of the gun. I went out of my body a little. I was blind and dizzy again. My stomach upended. I felt my hand levitate and something hard go into it. This was Paulie, putting the gun on my hand. I felt him over me, talking in my ear.

"Say something dramatic. Like you're in a movie. Something like, 'If I can't have you, no one will.'"

The phone. If I could get to the phone, I could blow up the truck. If I could blow up the truck, there would be enough of a distraction to get away. Or he'd run away. Or Antonio would wake up if he had a breath of life in him. Anything was better than this.

"Irene wants you," I rasped, blinking blood from my eye. "She told me in the bathroom."

The grip of his hand over mine loosened. I didn't have much control over my limbs, with half my brain checked out, but I pulled and yanked against all resistance, from his hand, the floor, the wall. The advantage was enough, and I got away.

The phone. Face down. There. I dove for it, but Paulie put his foot on it.

"She said what?"

"She said I could have Antonio. She was fighting for you." My fingertips touched the phone.

He moved it an inch farther. "Why should I believe you?"

And why should he? I drew lines and connections in my mind and, through the haze, found an answer that could buy me time.

"She texted me to meet her there. In the bathroom. To tell me." I lurched for the phone, and he shifted it another inch. "I'll show you."

He paused, standing above me, considering.

"I have no idea what she sees in you," I said. "So don't ask."

He smiled down at me. "If I see one tap on that glass I don't like…" He moved his foot. I grabbed the phone and pressed the home button for one, two…

Three seconds.

Four.

Five.

Paulie tilted his head, watching.

Six seconds on the home button.

Nothing exploded.

On seven, he knew there were no texts, and I knew there was no bomb. He kicked the phone from my hand.

"Worthless." He dropped on me, knee first, knocking the wind out of me, and wrestled the gun into my hand. He pointed it at Antonio. I tried to wiggle away, but he had me under his weight.

Antonio gasped and heaved, getting up on his elbows. I croaked his name and he turned.

"Say goodbye." Paulie squeezed my hand around the trigger.

Antonio rolled, and as if consciousness was equivalent to utter situational awareness and agility, he was on his back with his gun at Paulie's head as the pressure on my hand became enough for the trigger. A bullet lodged itself into the floor where Antonio's head had been. Every surface on my body got red hot as I realized I'd almost shot him.

"You're aiming over my head," Paulie said, taking my moment of surprise and using it to shift the gun back to Antonio. His hands were hot on mine, and once Antonio rolled, the sweat poured off them despite his cocky words. "You got blood in your fucking eye."

"Let her go, Paulie."

"When you're dead, brother. When you're out of my way. You been a drag on me from day one, and I've had it." He squeezed my hand. My palms were dead dry. How did I do that? How was my body an icebox in the face of so much menace?

But Paulie's hands were greased, strong and slick with sweat. I fought against him, and he tried to force me to shoot Antonio, moving the barrel across the room when his target moved. The pressure was too much. The trigger snapped, Antonio rolled, and a bullet landed in the wall in a *pop* of plaster dust.

Antonio's gun went flying and a line of blood opened up on his arm. The bullet had grazed him before hitting the wall.

I screamed, and an ice-cold, thoughtless panic took hold, because that man was my only chance at life, my one last gift of happiness and intimacy, and I'd shot him. I couldn't feel myself breathing.

Paulie moved me with Antonio, so the gun stayed pointed at him. But he had to move his elbow off my shoulder to do it, and I yanked myself away. His hands slid over mine, and I twisted, the pressure on the trigger still hard enough to discharge the gun. I took out a lamp.

Paulie and Antonio dove for Antonio's fallen weapon, and Antonio lost, rolling away as Paulie stood and pointed his gun at him.

"How do you like this, you fucking dago wop motherfucker?"

Antonio had his hands up, sitting akimbo, one shoulder to the wall. "You do this, you're going to have to answer for it."

"Fuck you!" he moved the gun when he spoke with his hands, pointing at his ex-partner with his unladen hand. "You leave us, you leave me, for her, and who answers for it. Huh? You don't. You dropped everything we had for a little pussy."

"We had business."

"Business? I loved you!" He blurted it out, and before he even got to the third word, I saw the shock and horror on his face.

He wouldn't let Antonio live after admitting that. It was all over his face. And after half a heartbeat, his body responded, leveling the gun at Antonio and pulling the trigger.

"No!" I heard my voice but didn't feel the shout in my breath. I swung to Paulie and squeezed my weapon. And after the very raw memory of almost shooting the man I loved, I did something in the ice-cold emotionless place I dwelled in.

I knew what I was doing.

It was not an accident.

And as if he saw my intention on my face, Antonio yelled my name.

But it was too late. Of my volition, I squeezed my fist more tightly, by an infinitesimal amount, and shot Paulie in the head. A bloom of red broke out under his wide-open eyes, and his head thunked down.

Sweat broke out in my palms, and the gun clanked to the floor, splashing in the growing, comma-shaped pool of blood.

My corruption was complete.

chapter 46.

ANTONIO

I moved, and he missed. And when he went down, it took me a second to realize why.

I played at standing straight, but my eyes had fog in front of them, and my balance was uneven. Even with my senses at fifty percent, I knew what was happening, and I gathered what dexterity I had to stand. To yell her name. Then, I had to hope she'd missed, even at a meter from his face.

Theresa, my Contessa, who stood straight and aimed her words like arrows, didn't miss. I didn't know it from the drop of Paulie's body because I wasn't looking at that. I was looking at her, only her. My grace. My sweet olive blossoms rotting on the branch.

She dropped the gun, and the sound cleared my mind.

I scooped it up.

"Capo," she whispered. Whatever cold, collected woman had shot Paulie was gone, and she shook from elbows to fingertips, eyes wide, lips parted. She had a sentence to finish, but apparently not the breath to do it.

"Get back to the truck," I said, putting my hands all over the gun. "Be seen. Wait. Just wait. For once…"

I sounded angry. Maybe I was. I grabbed the gun by the trigger and pointed it at Paulie, who looked like a mannequin. A bleeding one. The blood still poured out of him. He wasn't dead.

Gesù Cristo; that man was always thick. I used to think it was funny. I used to think it was good to be the brains of the operation.

He was impulsive. Stupid.

And I was muddled.

He'd helped me. He had a big heart that hurt. He'd helped me do wrong and right, and of course, he'd made everything balanced in an unbalanced world for a little while.

What was happening to me? I straightened my arm to finish him off. Behind me, Theresa sniffed. I turned. Her face was wet with tears, and the careful makeup she'd done for the wedding was smeared down her cheeks. She pressed her lips together.

Would shooting him save her? Would it make her happy and bind her to me, or would it break her?

That was my only concern: how it would affect Theresa, her heart and her life. I didn't even care if it would make her love me less, because it didn't matter anymore.

"Don't leave me," she whispered, her mouth wet with tears. "Please."

I wanted to say I'd never leave her, to hold her shoulders and say the thought had never crossed my mind. I wanted to say I'd never lied or snuck around or given up on her. But I had. In the guise of making her life easier, I had.

"I have to." I dropped the gun on the floor. It was stained with my prints. The whole mess would land in my lap, but I'd be dead, gone, and she couldn't step in the way of it. "Tell them you were hit in the head. Unconscious for the whole thing."

"Don't." Her voice was no more than a breath.

"You probably have a concussion." My voice was hard and distant. I didn't know how else to speak to her. She'd shot a man. She'd swung her arm to aim at him and squeezed the trigger. Her face had been as cold and hard as my voice, and she made no mistakes about the gun being loaded. She knew, and she'd shot to kill. Would I see anything else from now on?

"Were you seen coming in here?" I asked.

"Maybe? Probably? I don't know."

"Go back to the truck. They'll be here soon." I didn't want her to see me go to the closet. She knew where the tunnel was better than I did. "Go."

"There was no C4 under the chassis."

"Just go!"

"You think you're leaving without me."

"I was, I am…" I looked over Paulie's slow bleed then back at her.

We had to move.

No. *I* had to move.

I was leaving to protect her. She didn't have so much thrown at her that she couldn't manage. Daniel would never prosecute her if I were out of the picture. I was the one with the problems. I was the man with the baggage, and she was…

She wasn't innocent. Not anymore. Not with her running mascara and red eyes. Not with the bruise bubbling above her ear, or her grass-stained dress, or the powder burns on her hand.

I prayed God would forgive me for loving her, and feared only the devil would answer.

I picked up the gun and put it in my waistband.

"Antonio, no. I—"

"*Basta*," I said, opening the closet door. "I love you, Contessa. Your madness is silent and your sanity makes a racket. Now is time for madness." I pushed the hangers out of the way.

I found the false wall where she and her brother had described it. I ran my fingers over the edges but couldn't find a way to open it. She came up behind me, reaching between my legs and wedging her fingers into the corner between the floor and the wall.

"You have to go where children can reach." She pulled, and the false wall shifted. I took the edges from her. We were hit by a blast of air that should have been stale and dusty but wasn't. I knew she noticed from the deep breath she took.

She opened her mouth, and I sensed an objection coming out of it.

"Listen to me. I bought it the way I bought everything. It's not traceable. And yes, I was going down this tunnel. Alone. And I was never coming back. That was the plan, but it changed. I have to get something, and I will come back in a few seconds."

I put my finger to her lips. We had no time for explanations. "Be mad," I said. "Your sanity is there."

I ducked into the tunnel and down the stairs.

chapter 47.

THERESA

I must have been crazy. I'd intuited that he was leaving me when I was under the truck and couldn't lift the grate. No one could. It had been locked or bolted since I was a kid. And the C4 smelled like Play-Doh, which was made of wheat. C4 couldn't smell the same. Wheat didn't explode.

Stupida.

Standing in front of the tunnel with the fresh air coming from the other side, probably the result of Antonio reopening the basement, his plan became clear. He was going to leave me there and escape through the tunnel across Ludwig without me. But Paulie intervened. Damn Paulie, and bless him, because without him, I'd be under the truck, waiting like a good girl.

Paulie bled in the other room. I steeled myself against the horror of what I'd done. If I stood in that dark closet another minute, the steel was going to melt, and my madness wasn't going to be so silent.

I stepped into the abyss. It led to a wooden stairwell with steps higher than they were wide. I remembered that.

I put my other foot on the step.

He'd said to wait under the truck, and I hadn't done it.

I should wait now.

God, please let him come back to me.

Let.

Him.

Come.

Back.

Please.

I waited, and because I waited, I heard them coming. Maybe someone had heard shots, or maybe they'd seen the break-in of the florist's truck without a loving couple rocking the back. Maybe Daniel's minions went looking for me to thank and, discovering I wasn't there, came looking. I didn't know. But I knew there was a traitor's body in that room, and I knew I didn't want to explain what had happened.

I closed the closet door and shut the panel behind me.

It was pitch black, and if I remembered the stairs correctly, they were treacherous and rotted.

"Antonio," I whispered into the darkness. Was he gone?

Above me, I heard the clopping and shouting of people entering the carriage house and doing what needed doing. I wondered if they knew about the tunnels and whether there was someone from my world who would check.

My fingers grazed the stone walls. I'd seen them in the light. They were made of big rocks, cut into cross sections of multifaceted dark-grey ovals and mortared together with beige cement. To the hand they were rough and sharp, not cut but cracked.

Prepared to be in the tunnel under the grate, I snapped my keys from my bag and juggled to find the little LED light. I clicked it.

The service tunnel was five feet wide with a concrete floor cracked to dust and rock. The ceiling joists were thick, bare wood under slats and below them, Antonio stood, pointing a gun at me. His head had stopped bleeding, and in his other hand, he held a silver suitcase.

"Theresa," he said, lowering the gun.

"Antonio? Where are you going?"

"On my way back." He must have seen me look at the suitcase, because he held it up for me to see. "This is the C4."

"They're coming."

He looked up as if that would help him hear through the dirt and wood above. The thumping of booted feet and shouts of serious men came through the layers of ceiling and floor.

"I was going to die in the house and escape through the tunnel, the long way, to Ludwig, while you were safe under the truck."

I stepped toward him, my LED moving the shadows across his face. "We have to do your plan, but with two."

He pressed his lips together and looked down. He took my hand. "Si," he said. "We will."

A shout echoed over the walls, and he and I jerked our heads up. It was close, but not so close. In the closet maybe. Maybe they'd opened the door.

I felt his breath on me, short and shallow, and his eyes were a little wider under his bloody forehead. I put my hand over my mouth.

"Adesso!" he snipped, "And put the light out."

I did. He tugged me with him into the darkness. I tripped and he yanked me up. "A little ways, and I'll put the suitcase at the halfway point between the end and the closet stairs. Then we run." We came to a point where glass insets in the sidewalk let a little illumination through. It was night, and the spots of blue lamplight made more shadow than brightness.

"If people are coming, by the time we get there… we have to give up."

He jerked me forward, until the only barrier to me falling was his body. "I. Don't. Give. Up. Any. More." He said it through his teeth.

"I don't want to kill anyone else today."

In the dimmest of light, his brow shading his expression, he whispered, "I can plant it here, before they come down. There will be a bomb between us and them, but we need to be protected."

"There's a well," I said. "Fiona used to throw her empty vials down there."

I didn't give him a chance to answer. It was my turn to yank him to where we had to go, clicking my little light on when it got too dark to see. I pulled him through a room with a ditch that smelled of dried meat and over to a rotted-wood platform with a water pump. It keened to the side.

I found the rusted iron ring in the center and pulled up a wooden circular lid. Antonio shone his light down it. It was dry as a bone, and smaller than I remembered, with no vials, as if someone, some kid or some adult hiding something, had filled it in.

"Plant the bomb behind the wall and—"

"Get in," Antonio growled, dropping the suitcase.

"But you won't fit."

He knocked my feet from under me and caught me, carrying me in both arms, and as effortlessly as he did everything, he put me into the hole.

It was a tight fit. I couldn't fit a kitten in there with me, much less Antonio.

"Two explosions," he said. "Wait for them both. Then come through the house across Ludwig Street."

"Where will you be?"

"There."

Shouting, close by. Voices on stone. They'd found the partition and moved it. I thought we'd have more time. There was no chance he would get close enough to the closet to block the way and then back to safety in time.

"You have to detonate now," I said. "Before they come down. You'll never make it."

"Two explosions. Wait. Then get out and run to the house. The car is in the back. Don't stop until you're in the car."

"Wait!"

"I have to put this thing by the stairs, back there, to keep them from coming down. No more delays."

Before I could answer, he slammed the lid back on. Darkness. Silence.

I knew the distances all too well. The halfway point between the well and the house, under the street, was too far for him to get to, and that suitcase would blow in some cop or security guard's face. If he left it close to where we were, the time it would take for him to get to safety would cause the same result.

He would die. And in the middle of the realization, the explosion hit. The earth seemed to move against me on the left and expand away on the right.

He couldn't have gotten away. No one could run that fast.

I wanted to get out. I needed to see where he was, but I had to wait, and the second explosion came on the heels of the first. I cringed because it came so fast.

I didn't wait a second longer than I had to. I shook the ringing out of my ears and put my hands against the trapdoor. It was red hot, and I snapped my palms back with a curse.

Closing my eyes and steeling myself, breathing, counting three, two, one...

I punched the wood. The burning sensation was nothing compared to the hardness of the surface against my inexperienced hands. But it moved, just a little, shifting to the ledge and over. I saw the room above in the crescent of space between the well edge and the lid, bathed in flickering red light and letting in a blast of heat.

I shifted and wedged my foot above me, pushing at the lid with the soles of my feet, and kicked upward. The lid creaked and shifted, the circle breaking at the diameter. Beyond it, the ceiling smoked. I scrambled out of the hole, careful not to touch anything that could have been hot.

The air was scorching and the smoke thick enough to burn my eyes and throat. I crouched and got out of the room and into the service hall.

There, I saw the origin of the fire, where the hundred-year-old roof beams burned and the smoke was thicker than sour cream. It was closer to the carriage house, as if Antonio had actually walked back the way we'd come to set the bomb off, which would have made his way back to the house even longer.

Could he have made it to the house, between closing me up and the explosion? I tried to remember how long the interval had been. Ten seconds?

I couldn't think about it, but as I scuttled to the house across Ludwig Street, digging into the recesses of my memory to recall the way, the seconds ticked, and I knew there was no way in hell he'd made it. No.

He'd planted the bomb near the carriage house to block whomever was on the way down.

Pockets of fire raged in the corners, and smoke billowed in angry curls. My chest burned, my feet found every fracture and crack in the ground, and the heat felt like it was blasting at my back until I eventually found the end of the tunnel to the house across the street.

The door was ancient and heavy. My eyes burned so badly I couldn't do more than feel for the hundred-year-old knob and deadbolt. They were hot to the touch, and I cursed. I picked up my skirt and shielded my right hand with the fabric then licked my left hand and quickly turned the deadbolt. I opened the door and closed it behind me. The air in the stairwell seemed seven hundred degrees cooler. I took it in as if I'd never breathed before, and my lungs punished me by feeling as though they were being stabbed with every gasp.

After a couple of blinks, I looked up. The stairs were the same as they'd always been, and at the top was a rough-hewn oval where Antonio had broken through the wall.

Antonio.

Fuck.

I ran up the stairs. Tripped. Fell. Got the hell up. I ran again and reached the dark basement, falling palms-first onto sharp plaster chips. I screamed. It hurt badly. I looked down, and even though I couldn't see well past my singed eyes and the room's darkness, it was obvious my hands were burned.

I swallowed. That hurt, too. It had been worse than I'd remembered down there. I'd been intent on getting out, getting to Antonio. I hadn't even known I was in hell. And where was he? Was he still down there? What if he was burning to death on the far side of the tunnel, and I was up here with my feet on cold plaster, waiting?

I thought about going back down. I saw myself wandering through ten miles of tunnel, calling his name. I knew I shouldn't have let him put me in that well. I shouldn't have let him close the lid or walk away or any of it. I should have protected him the way he protected me.

And that was what he'd done. He'd protected me every step of the way. He'd put me under the umbrella of his love, and I'd done nothing but stand in his way. I'd made it my business to assert myself, and in doing so, I'd put him between me and death.

"Antonio." I whispered, but no one answered. I didn't even know who I was calling to in that dark basement. He wasn't there. He couldn't have made it and closed the door behind him. It was just me, with a murder on my conscience and my docket, on the run, alone.

Don't stop until you're in the car.

"Get it together," I said to myself. I could cry about Antonio another day. Today, I had to make his death worthwhile. I breathed, even though it hurt, and looked over the basement. One stairwell went up to the house; I knew that. A blast of cold air came from another shorter, rough-hewn exit that led right outside. I heard the sirens through that opening and went to it.

The fresh air hit my face like a Freon blast. The yard went back a hundred feet and was surrounded by cinderblock and cast iron. A white car waited by the exit, which led to a back alley. I couldn't tell the make, but it was nondescript, looking like a million other cars in the city. I walked to it, wondering how I was going to open the door without bloodying the handle or drive without touching the wheel. And then, ten steps in, I berated myself for worrying about my stupid problems after what had just happened, and I had to fight an emptiness and uncertainty I'd never felt before. The plan had been to go to Tijuana then drive south to Guatemala, and fly to Greece under different names. I couldn't remember if I'd promised to stick to the plan. Was it the right thing to do? Did it even matter without him? I put my head on the cool roof of the car, listening to the sirens a block away. I prayed that no one was hurt, that I could gather the strength to drive away alone, and that Antonio was in heaven.

The smell of burning wood that saturated my clothes reminded me of him, and I decided I'd never wash that fucking dress. We'd tried everything together. We'd done crazy things, wild, irresponsible shit. My God, I'd shot someone. I was a murderer for the rest of my life. I'd killed two men: Paulie, on purpose, and Antonio through sheer recklessness.

My breath hitched, and though I tried to hold back the tears, they came nonetheless. A minute to cry. I had to just take a minute to breathe, mourn, and cry.

Like angelic comfort from the firmament, a hand
came on my shoulder.

It was a cop, maybe, or some other authority figure
come to arrest me, or Daniel gently comforting me
before handing me over for a hundred infractions.
Then I felt a hand on the other shoulder, and through
the smell of burning wood that saturated my clothes,
hiding all other scents, came a voice.

"Passenger side, Contessa."

I spun so quickly I got dizzy and fell into
Antonio's arms. I was saved, pulled from the jaws of
despair. I didn't care why or how, just that it was true
that he was with me.

"What? Theresa? What's wrong?" He pushed me
away, and when he saw I cringed, he looked down. My
hands were up, in front of me. He took them from
underneath.

"*Gesù*, what happened?"

"I thought you were dead," I said.

His ripped shirtsleeve dangled off his elbow like
bunting. "Not yet. I run faster than you think." He held
his finger to my face, first pointing then stroking the
length of my nose. "But next time we go to a wedding,
the worst that will happen is you get too drunk to
dance."

"I don't drink at weddings."

He put the hand without the ripped shirtsleeve on
my cheek and kissed me in the dark yard, with the
crickets squeaking their mating call and the *thup-thup-thup* of the helicopters getting closer.

"You ready to go?" his mouth whispered into mine before he kissed me. God, I couldn't believe I thought I'd lost that hungry mouth, those lips, soft with intention, framing a brutal tongue. I couldn't touch him because my hands were still raw and burned, but he pulled me closer in that kiss. I wanted him to tear me apart against the side of that nondescript white car.

But I pushed the kiss off before I could ask and he could be tempted to comply. "You driving, Capo?" I barely had enough breath to finish the sentence.

"*Si, amore mio.*"

He walked me to the passenger side and held the door open for me. His arm was bloody under the torn shirt, but he didn't say a word about it. He knocked on the hood of the car as he came around, as if sending me a message that everything was all right and that he had it under control, and when he got in and the gate opened, I knew he did.

The car pulled into the street, and we drove south, to our life.

epilogue.

THERESA

Tijuana was filthy. A year ago, I would have been happy to leave because of that alone. The heat, even in December, the layer of crud on everything, the narrow alleys that smelled of piss, and the stink of old tequila and beer in the air would have been enough to get me on a plane early.

We had no phones, no way to be contacted. We were gone. Poof. Disappeared. I never felt so free in my life.

"Terrified," I said to Antonio. He looked as if a layer of worry had been scraped from him. He looked younger, even.

"Fear is a good thing," he replied, leaning over the bar, tilting his glass bottle on the bar surface, leaving an arc of condensation behind. We'd stopped in a small hotel that looked as if it was going to give up any minute and collapse into a pile of wood and dust. "Keeps you honest."

I hadn't been afraid when we'd crossed over the border into Mexico. He'd packed clothes and cash and hid his wounded arm under a sleeve. It hadn't been so bad, nothing a little unguent and a kiss couldn't fix. My hands had second-degree burns, and though they looked awful, I only had to fold them to hide them. I had nothing. He thought I wasn't coming, so I had only the clothes on my back, the crap in my bag, and some valuables I wouldn't part with.

We'd crossed the border when the traffic was so dense we would have only gotten stopped if blood were dripping from the trunk. Then we made it a point to laugh and joke as we went through Border Patrol, as if we were no more than a loving couple looking for a fun weekend. I think we were so high on adrenaline that nothing was easier than manic laughter.

The explosion had made the news immediately. It had been contained in the tunnel. The report stated no deaths and one injury.

"They're not saying we're dead," I'd said.

"It's been an hour," he'd replied, but he furrowed his brow.

"I saw that tunnel. Nothing would have survived it."

"Things happened we didn't expect. Our exit wasn't clean."

"I'll go back and die again," I said.

He laughed and drove the Toyota safely and sanely southward. I talked when I didn't want to think about my family. I knew my memories of them would cloud and get distant until I could only remember little things. I played with the radio, and before we even hit San Diego, the news of Daniel Brower's collapse as mayoral candidate hit the airwaves.

The TV was on in the bar, hanging above us, blaring Spanish, the light shining through the miasma of cheap Honduran cigarettes. Antonio could only decipher some of the news, but the pictures told the story. They showed an Italian wedding, joyful yet staid, and a room full of people, each with a story, each living a different version of the events until suddenly, arrows were superimposed on the screen, pointing at three men in suits.

As one, they whipped off earpieces as if in pain.

"What happened?" I asked.

He leaned his back on the bar, looking very pleased with himself. "When you pressed your home key..."

"No bomb. Thanks for that."

"They got their wires from the bathroom attendant. Then you put this radio signal out. A very loud, high-pitched squeak. Very loud. His little team was exposed. He looks like the ass he is."

I must have gotten sullen. My face, which hid everything from everyone else, was pure bright-yellow signage to him. It always had been. From the minute he beat some guy on the hood of a car, he'd known what I was feeling.

He put his fingertips on my chin. "It was for your own good."

"You didn't want to fight for us. You were just going to leave."

"I didn't want you to spend your life fighting. I want life to be easy for you. I want you to be happy. If I humiliated him, and he lost the election, he'd back off troubling you. I'd be gone. You'd be happy. That's all I ever wanted. More than wanting you for myself, I want you to have a good life."

"If it hadn't worked out the way it had—"

"Don't."

"Are you upset that we're here, together?" I asked.

"I'm upset that you scarred your soul for me. That's the biggest sin I live with."

"That's not what I asked." I looked at my orange juice then at the specks of pulp on the side of the glass, as if they could help me divine what he was thinking.

"Theresa," he whispered then drifted off.

"Never mind," I said, waving it off. "It is what it is. I think I'm just tired." I shut down. I didn't want to talk anymore. I wanted to pretend everything was perfect. If we'd been alone together I would have taken my clothes off and tried to drown my sorrow in pain and pleasure.

But being let off the hook wasn't going to fly with him, not for one second. He put his beer down and took my head in his hands, thumbs on my cheeks and fingers at the back of my head. "Listen to me, and listen very, very carefully. We have a difficult list of things to do, and I need you to be the woman you are, the woman who can run the world. So, I'm going to say this once. Are you listening?"

He was so intense, so close. He couldn't lie or obfuscate from that distance. "Yes, Capo."

"I didn't dream of this moment. I did try to leave you, but it was for your own good. I wanted to free you. I admit I was ready to walk away. And I admit that when you shot Paulie, I decided you had to come with me to protect yourself from being accused of his murder. I had to tell myself I was protecting you. But, my Contessa, I was so happy to be forced. I felt it was a gift. I had an excuse to take you and have everything I wanted. I can't lie to myself. Yes, I want to protect you from being hurt, but I just want you. Plain and simple."

"Antonio, You've been trying to get away from me since the minute we met. If you do it again, it will be the last time. My heart can't take it."

He nodded, looking at the bar surface. "I didn't dream God could make it possible for me to have you. But He made it impossible for it to happen in any other way. Do you see what that means? It means I was destined to defile you. I live with that every day. My destiny is to destroy."

"Maybe I was destined to be destroyed."

"*Shh.* Listen. I want you to have a normal, sweet life, but I can't give you that. I will never be that man for you. Never. But here you are, with me. I am happy, and I carry the weight of my guilt for that happiness. So, don't fool yourself; I don't just want you, I hunger for you. My skin needs your skin against it. My mouth needs to taste your mouth. I. Am. Happy. But my soul has never been so stained."

I swallowed a tablespoon of gunk. "I'm sorry," I said through my tears. "I've made such a mess."

"I forgive you. Can you forgive me?"

"I love you. You are my only, my one and only. And if I have to turn my life upside down, or go to hell to be with you, so be it."

"That's not to be undertaken lightly."

"It never was. Never," I said.

His eyes scanned mine as if deciphering the full meaning of the message: that I'd always understood what being with him meant and had grabbed it with both hands from the beginning. I never shared his doubts, and I think, for once, that comforted rather than troubled him.

"If I ask you this, I want you to answer it after you think about it. Don't rush."

"Ask what?"

He breathed lightly, almost a sigh, then brushed his fingers over my cheek. "Will you be my wife?"

"Yes."

"I told you not to rush."

"I'll tell you again tomorrow. Same thing. Yes, yes, yes."

We crashed together, mouths open, lips entangled, arms tightening around each other for the first moments of commitment, nothing between us but love.

The bartender wiped around our glasses, whistling. Antonio held my face fast to him then kissed my cheek and whispered in my ear, "I just heard your name on the news. They aren't sure we're dead."

"We failed, then?"

"We were only buying time. We need to go."

"No time for a good-bye-to-Tijuana screw?"

"Plenty of time for that later," he said.

I smiled, imagining "later." His body was mine, and I watched it move as he put a few bills on the bar and pulled me toward the door, every finger a lightning rod for my desire. I took a glance at the TV and jerked him to a stop. He followed my gaze up there.

Jonathan's name was in the little tape below a reporter who stood outside Sequoia hospital.

"What is she saying?" I thought I was speaking in a normal voice, but I barely breathed it. I scoured my mind. Had Jonathan been at the wedding and I didn't know it? Had he been hurt by something I'd done?

"Something went wrong. The heart, like you said," Antonio said, knotting his brow as he deciphered a language he only partly understood. He pressed his lips together the way he did when he was reluctant to say something. "It's bad." Antonio shook his head. "I don't know all the medical words, but they say he will die."

The TV flipped to a *futbol* game, and the bar patrons cheered. The room suddenly smelled sweatier, wetter, and more florid than it had.

"I like your brother," Antonio said.

I didn't answer. I didn't have words. I had only a dead weight in my chest where a light heart should have been. I couldn't swallow. I couldn't feel my fingertips. Where had my elation gone, and my need for Antonio and only Antonio? Was it that easily swept away?

"We'll keep the news on in the car," I said. "Maybe they'll say something else."

I walked out into the heavy heat of the street. It was December, and I was sweating. The concrete flower boxes and indecipherable color-soaked graffiti that had charmed me on the way in seemed to mock me now, and the bent street with its dented cars no longer spoke of a charming over use but instead invoked an angry entropy, a sick god of destruction. The plaster cracks over every inch of the city twisted themselves into a net that wanted to catch me and drag me away from Antonio.

"I want to go somewhere with winters," I said when he caught up to me. "Can we do that? Can we live somewhere with snow?"

"You need to go back."

"No!" I shouted it to block out the knowledge that I needed to go, more than anything. I'd underestimated the pull of my family. I'd left them as if they'd always be the same, for the something different that Antonio embodied, and they changed as soon as I turned my back.

A man in a straw hat, one of many passing us, turned to watch as he walked.

"I can't do anything about it," I said, slashing with my arms. "I can't donate my heart. I'm using it."

He took me by the wrists stilling them. "Contessa, my love. He's your brother."

"I can't. I made a choice. I chose *you*."

"And I chose you. I am yours. You are mine. I'm going to make you my wife and steal your name from under you. But if you turn your back on your family, you won't forgive yourself if he dies—"

"Don't say that!"

"It's a reality," he said.

"I'll forgive myself fine. I can turn my back on my brother because I can't help him. He doesn't need me. My presence is meaningless."

He paused, looking across the street at the *putt-putt*ing, half-functioning cars and the stacked stucco buildings. Then he looked back at me. "I won't let you take the rap for Paulie."

"Are you serious?" I said. "You think I'm letting you take the blame for that?"

"My prints are on the gun. You will not go to jail for Paulie, as God is my witness."

"You brought me here to keep me from taking that rap, and now you—"

"No," he said. "I brought you because I love you. Because I need you. Because heaven gave me a reason to have you."

"And what about Irene? And Donna Maria?"

"I didn't promise you this would be easy. It's ten times worse now."

He shook his head as if he wanted to say things and didn't, as if words wanted to tumble out, and he held back the tide. I balled my fists and steeled myself for a fight. Jonathan had six more sisters and two living parents to care for him. A prodigal sister wasn't necessary. If I went to see him, it would be for me, not him, and despite what Antonio might think, I wasn't feeling selfish.

"If this happened in twenty years," I said, "when it was supposed to, we could slip back without a problem, and I could see him. If we go back today, we destroy everything."

He held his hands out. "Isn't that what we do?"

I wanted to cry with frustration. I shook my head, looking into the traffic, the noise, the bedlam we had more than embraced. We'd gotten on the cliff of normalcy and jumped into the chaos face first. Of course, that was what we did. I couldn't deny it anymore.

"I don't want to," I said.

"He's your brother."

"And damn him for it."

Antonio kissed me slowly in the fetid heat, and I tasted the sweat of his cheek, the beer on his tongue. His lips were a promise, a blood bond, a kiss of greeting and good-bye, and the years in between.

"I won't let anything happen to you, Capo," I said.

"I know."

"Are you sure about this?"

"Yes." He sighed and looked up, as if seeing the narrow street for the first time. "I smell the beach."

"Let's walk on it," I said. "We can decide what to do together."

He slipped his arm around my neck, and we walked to the end of the block. The beach was a right turn and a few blocks away. We traversed it three times before our plan was set, and then, as if it was our job to dive headfirst into chaos and ruin, we began.

ruin.

Fine, per adesso.

Though the Downtown Gate Club is a figment of my imagination, there are tunnels under Downtown Los Angeles. Because they are closed to the public, I went to the tunnels in Pendleton, Oregon for my research. My LA underground is based on those. Any actual differences with the actual LA tunnels are just too damn bad. I do my best with what I've got.

I anticipate three total in the series, and I may need up to eight months between them.
The best way to find out when the next book is out is to sign up for the mailing list at cdreiss.com

To find out when the next book is coming out, sign up for the mailing list at cdreiss.com.

Have you read the *Songs of Submission*?
No?
Because Theresa's brother, Jonathan has this whole thing happening with Monica, that singer with the short-circuiting mouth, and it's all kinds of epic length. Links and reading order below:

Songs of Submission, Sequence One
1) Beg
2) Tease
3) Submit

Songs of Dominance
Very short, optional read
3.5) Jessica/Sharon

Songs of Submission, Sequence Two
4) Control
5) Burn
6) Resist

Songs of Dominance
Very short, optional read between Burn and Resist
5.5) Rachel

Songs of Submission, Sequence Three
7) Sing

Songs of Dominance
7.5) Monica - a very short story, is the last of it, and you might need it after *Sing*.

If you prefer saving a couple of dollars, and feel ok committing to a few books at a time, the bundles might work for you.
Sequence One - books 1-3 Beg/Tease/Submit
Sequence Two - books 4-6 Control/Burn/Resist

Fiona Drazen's life as a celebutante and submissive slave in *Songs of Perdition* starts with KICK. It's available everywhere. It's a serial, so expect short books, every few months, as other projects allow. Book two, USE is also out.

Thanks to my team, the Canaries, Team Drazen, all my goddesses and kings There are so many bloggers who help me I can't even mention all of them without missing ten. Kaylee, Jean, Lisa, Tony, Diana, Eva, Christy. Thank you.

Gabri Canova helped with the Italian phrasing in the story. Thank you, Goddess.
Erik Gevers did the formatting, yet again making me look like a pro.

My family tolerates me, and I love them so much. D-Sleepy, A-Bomb, Lady Nono.

Ciao.

Made in the USA
San Bernardino, CA
12 October 2014